He watched as Tabitha's mouth quirked into a grin.

"I've experienced a bit of the same while in school, so I can understand. In light of that, I suggest we call a truce." She held out a delicate hand, covered with small scrapes. "You can call me Tab."

He tugged her toward his site. "Well, c'mon with me, Tab, and let me fix up those scrapes before they get infected." When she started to hesitate, he waved toward the mass of baggage stacked behind them. "Or do you know where your medical supplies are in all that mess?"

She surprised him with a spontaneous, sultry laugh. "I don't know where any specific bag or box is in all that mess; let alone what's in each one. I'll take advantage of your kind offer in light of the truce."

Hunter clasped her delicate wrist and felt a jolt shoot through him. He had the distinct feeling that the heavenly Father he'd prayed to earlier now chuckled at him in the same way Hunter had chuckled at Tab. The unnerving thought that nothing in his world would ever be the same slowly drifted across his mind.

PAIGE WINSHIP DOOLY enjoys living in the warm panhandle of Florida with her family, after having grown up in the sometimes extremely cold Midwest. She is happily married to her high school sweetheart, Troy, and they have six homeschooled children. Their oldest son, Josh, now lives in Colorado, while the newest blessing, Jetty, rounds out the family in a wonderful way. The whole family is active in Village Baptist Church. Paige has always loved to write. She feels her love of writing is a blessing from God, and she hopes that readers will walk away with a spiritual impact on their lives and smiles on their faces.

Books by Paige Winship Dooly

HEARTSONG PRESENTS
HP84—Heart's Desire
HP775—Treasure in the Hills

The Greatest Find

Paige Winship Dooly

Heartsong Presents

A note from the Author:
I love to hear from my readers! You may correspond with me by writing:

Paige Winship Dooly
Author Relations
PO Box 721
Uhrichsville, OH 44683

ISBN 978-1-60260-058-4

THE GREATEST FIND

All scripture quotations are taken from the King James Version of the Bible.

All of the characters and events in this book are fictitious. Any resemblance to actual persons, living or dead, or to actual events is purely coincidental.

Our mission is to publish and distribute inspirational products offering exceptional value and biblical encouragement to the masses.

PRINTED IN THE U.S.A.

one

Northeast Utah, 1900

Tabitha "Tab" Augustine clasped her hands together against the front of her chest and spun in a circle, taking in the sights and sounds of their newest dig. "Oh, Father, can you believe it? We're finally here in Utah, at one of the most exciting potential dinosaur digs ever. Just imagine! It's supposed to be a huge event, and we're a part of it. All our plans, our dreams—they're about to come to life. We might just win the award and even get the plaque in the Statford Museum with our names on it to record the momentous discovery!"

"*If* there's a discovery." Her father, Peter Augustine, stood next to her, silently taking in the activity before them.

Wagons from town deposited men and supplies at various tents, the horses shuffling nervously at the commotion and chaos. Near the "kitchen" area, men unloaded barrels of water from town—water that would be used for both drinking and bathing. Tab wrinkled her nose. She hated bathing without the benefit of a tub but had learned how to compensate after being dragged all over the world to primitive places by her father. A pail of water, a cloth, and sweet-smelling perfume made all the difference in the world in such a situation.

She turned her thoughts back to their quest. Whoever found the first significant dinosaur bone would be handsomely rewarded, both financially and with recognition. That fact had

5

dinosaur seekers from around the world converging upon the area.

Tabitha paced, stretching her legs after the long wagon ride with their gear. The excavation provided their transportation to the site, with a few horses available on the location for contestants' private use. The dig also provided scheduled wagon trips back and forth to Vernal for anyone needing a trip into town.

Tab continued on, ignoring her father's sour mood. "Just to be here is so amazing. We're a part of this find from the beginning, and if the mavericks"—Tab sent a disdainful glare in the direction of the free-spirited tent-dweller setting up not ten feet away from them—"if the mavericks can keep from decimating the site before we even get started, we have a chance to find the first specimen!"

Her father remained quiet, and she couldn't help but glance at their neighbor again. The blond-haired rogue, hands on hips, stared at them and actually mouthed the word *decimate* in slow motion, as if testing to see how the word—most surely foreign to his day-to-day vocabulary—settled upon his tongue.

Tab stared back with distaste and then turned away, but not before noticing the man tip his hat with a sarcastic flourish in her direction.

"Arrogant egomaniac," she muttered. *Let him look up those words in a dictionary.* She and her father had come across plenty of others like him in their day. His kind tended to be rough around the edges and weren't as educated in the field, a recipe for disaster. She'd never liked their style. Her father, a well-known archaeologist and world-renowned dinosaur excavator, had dragged her all over the world, always looking for the next great find. She'd seen plenty of men like the man across the way. She lowered her voice. "Father, why must they allow men like that into the competitions? You know they're only here for the glory, not for any scientific reason or to further mankind's knowledge."

Her father looked at her for the first time since their arrival only minutes earlier. "You know we want our name on that plaque every bit as much as the mavericks do." He sent Tabitha a smile, but the smile was tight and laced with bitterness and left Tabitha feeling like something was amiss.

Before she had a chance to question her father more deeply, the site coordinator appeared, walking briskly in their direction. Tabitha knew better than to bring up family business in front of others, so she filed away her concern for another time and turned to face the approaching man.

"Dr. Augustine." He lifted a hand in greeting and shook her father's hand. "I'm so pleased to meet you. And you must be Miss Augustine." He also tipped his hat, but with a genuineness that lacked the mocking nature of her neighbor's acknowledgment.

"Yes, sir, and I'm most excited to be here." Tabitha found herself reverting to the training in propriety that dated back to her preparatory school days. At one point, her father had worried over her all-consuming interest in science—an interest not considered ladylike at all—and had sent her to school near her grandmother's house in Boston, determined to make a proper lady out of her.

After Tab debated with several of the instructors about various teachings—and won—they insisted she didn't fit in at the academy and would be better suited completing her education in the field with her father. She hadn't meant to make them look inferior in front of their students, but when they taught incorrect information about places she'd personally visited, she felt it her duty to correct the misinformation.

"I'm Joey Matthews," the coordinator continued. "I'm sure you're familiar with who I am and my position here. I'm in charge of the site and will be happy to help with any concerns or questions."

Since Joey had sent correspondence with continuous updates during the previous few months while setting up details of the dig, she was sure every person here was familiar with his name and position. He'd apparently felt it important to include a staged photograph of himself in the original packet, posing against a huge skeleton of a dinosaur that had recently been found and transported to a prestigious museum back East.

Why did such men always seem to want unending affirmation from those around them? Tabitha's father was a doer. He'd taught her at a young age to go after what she wanted, and she didn't need anyone else's approval to get there.

When neither Augustine answered—her father still miles away in his musings and Tab unintentionally focused on dissecting the pompous man before them—Joey spoke up as if they hadn't missed the opportunity to stroke his needy ego.

"Well, you seem to have chosen your work location well. You have today and tomorrow to set up camp. If you need anything, don't hesitate to look me up. You'll find me somewhere around the dig at any given time."

Her father shook himself out of his deep thoughts and spoke before Joey could step away. "We'll do just that, Mr. Matthews. Thank you. And we're still meeting tomorrow night for a briefing of the rules and requirements, is that correct?"

"Please, call me Joey. We'll be working around each other for quite a while and might as well be comfortable. And yes, we'll meet right over there"—he pointed to an open area over his shoulder that had been kept clear of tents— "tomorrow night, just before sundown. The contest rules will be discussed, we'll have a group dinner, and you'll have a chance to get to know the other men you're competing against."

Tabitha didn't miss her father's scowl at the coordinator's words. "Thank you. We'll make sure to be there. See you then, Mr. Matthews. Joey." She quickly added the last when the man opened his mouth to correct her. Her act of familiarity was rewarded with a smile. She hid a shiver of disgust. Whether he liked it or not, she'd refer to him by his surname from here on out; she didn't want to falsely lead him on. Being the lone woman at most sites, male attention ended up, in all cases, being a hazard to her work. She tried hard to balance courtesy with aloofness, and this dark-haired smooth talker clued her in immediately that she'd do best to steer clear of him. She glanced again at her handsome blond neighbor. He waved. And she'd most definitely do well to steer clear of him, too.

ન

Hunter Pierce looked skyward and silently asked his heavenly Father what he'd done of late to merit having the only woman at the site no more than a horse's measure away from his tent. Women weren't even welcome at these events. But no one dared stand up to the well-known and much welcomed Dr. Peter Augustine and declare his daughter wasn't every bit as welcome. So wherever he went, she followed. A lot of men considered the very presence of a female a promise of bad luck to come.

Of course, Hunter didn't believe in luck, bad or good. He believed in a Higher Power and was proud to be a follower of Jesus. He chuckled and glanced at his new neighbors as he thought about how well-received that bit of knowledge always was with the scientific types. The topic would surely come up before the dig ended. Though he'd heard of the duo and had read about them and their extensive travels, he'd yet to come face-to-face with them on a dig—that is, until now.

He'd noticed during the past few minutes of his observation that the daughter, Tabitha, came across as both an exuberant young lady and a refined scientific scholar, a surprisingly attractive combination of traits. Now, as he watched, she began to dig wholeheartedly through the two trunks and boxes of gear that had been dropped off by the wagon master's crew. At least she didn't seem the pampered type who sat around complaining while her father did all the work. As a matter of fact, her father still stood and surveyed the work field in silence while his daughter jumped into action.

Hunter felt a small urge to offer his assistance but shook it off. His site was secure. He had worked all day to get things in place and set up. He'd had a goal to arrive early so he could decide on the best place to begin, and he'd followed through. The sun beat down warmly upon his head, and he needed to sit and put his feet up and relax a bit while he could. After tomorrow the days would be long and grueling. He deserved this time of rest. He pulled an empty crate over to the measly shade provided by the side of his tent, settled back into a hardwood chair he'd lugged along, pulled his worn hat over his face, and propped his feet up on the crate in front of him.

He closed his eyes and tried to relax, but Tabitha's grunts and oomphs were hard to ignore. He considered slipping into his tent for a little shut-eye, but with the heat bearing down on him even out in the slight breeze, he knew trying to sleep inside the hot enclosure would not do any good. Besides, the flimsy fabric would do nothing to block the sounds around him. And even though he hadn't slept well during any of the preceding nights before his arrival, he never had been one to stay idle for long. Sleeping during the day felt impossible to him.

He opened an eye, tipped his hat up with one finger, and peeked at his intriguing neighbor. He chuckled aloud as she wiped her lower arm across her forehead, leaving a streak of dirt on her previously pristine skin. Her own broad-brimmed leather hat, much like one a cowboy would wear, clung precariously to the back of her head. Wayward strands of curly blond hair had fallen loose and now framed the petite features of her face, which somehow made her seem more approachable and soft. How women ever coped with their long skirts in this heat had never ceased to amaze him. His mother and sisters worked long hours every day and so did all the other women he'd encountered. His chuckle earned him another dagger of a glare from the woman setting up camp across the hard-packed dirt. He quirked an amused eyebrow in response, much too hot and lazy to move, and crossed his arms over his chest.

A few moments later, Tabitha tugged at an unyielding bundle that suddenly yielded. The entire pile tumbled down on her. Immediately Hunter was on his feet and at her side, pulling the heavy objects away. Her father, as soon as he'd realized what had happened, belatedly joined in. If Hunter had expected warm comments of appreciation, he was way off. He'd have felt safer after freeing a wildcat as ferocious as she was when he held a hand out to help her to her feet.

"I suggest you maintain your distance and keep your dusty hands off me in the future if you don't want to feel the full effect of my wrath," she hissed.

She began to dust her skirts by slapping at them and fluffing them in the air. Hunter smirked as the action reminded him of the piglets back home in St. Louis after a roll in the mud. They'd soak in the rays, and when the mud dried, dust would fly in all directions from their bodies if a brisk wind blew up.

"I don't know what you find amusing. Surely you have better things to do than sit around and stare at me." She resumed her tirade even as she took stock of wounds or injuries. She turned her wrists this way and that and then did the same with her ankles. Her boots peeked out from under the hem of her long, dark blue skirt, but other than a bit of dust, all body parts seemed to have fared well while under the pile of crates. Everything but her temper seemed to be in good order.

Taking into consideration her present mood, he wasn't about to share his mental comparison of her and the piglets back home. He might not be the most scholarly man here, but he knew when to keep his mouth shut, at least most of the time.

"Maybe we should start over and properly introduce ourselves. I'm Hunter Pierce." Hunter offered her his hand, which she pointedly ignored. He dropped it to his side. "And you're Tabitha Augustine, if I recall correctly. I've read about you and your father."

Hunter turned to include the man in his spiel, but Tabitha's father had gone back into his funk, walking over to sit on a previously buried crate, once again watching the flurry of activity around them. The man certainly was a strange one.

Tab briefly glanced up at him. "Interesting how a life of studying science puts you, the scientist, under the same scrutiny your research goes through."

She had stopped her fussing and now stared past Hunter with a faraway look in her clear blue eyes. Her words were laced with pain, as if that scrutiny hadn't been kind. Or maybe she just didn't like writings of her private life being sent around the periodicals of the world. Up close, the woman became all softness, and her beauty literally took his breath away. She focused her full attention on him, her features reverting back to angry lines.

"While you've spent the past thirty minutes doing nothing but gawk at me, I've tried to put our camp in order. Have you nothing better to do than sit over there and laugh at me?" She crossed her arms defensively, but something akin to pain reflected in her eyes.

Hunter felt properly set in his place. If his mother were here, she'd ignore the fact that he was a grown man of twenty-eight and would take a green branch to his backside over his present behavior. "I'm sorry if I've offended you. That was not my intent. But you sent me some well-aimed barbs in the short time since your arrival. And unfortunately, my thoughts have always seemed to reflect openly on my face, much to my consternation, as far back as when I was a young lad in school. I have a way of getting myself into spots that I don't really mean to get into. Like now."

He watched as Tabitha's mouth quirked into a grin. "I've

experienced a bit of the same while in school, so I can understand. In light of that, I suggest we call a truce." She held out a delicate hand, covered with small scrapes. "You can call me Tab."

He tugged her toward his site. "Well, c'mon with me, Tab, and let me fix up those scrapes before they get infected." When she started to hesitate, he waved toward the mass of baggage stacked behind them. "Or do you know where your medical supplies are in all that mess?"

She surprised him with a spontaneous, sultry laugh. "I don't know where any specific bag or box is in all that mess, let alone what's in each one. I'll take advantage of your kind offer in light of the truce."

Hunter clasped her delicate wrist and felt a jolt shoot through him. He had the distinct feeling the heavenly Father he'd prayed to earlier now chuckled at him in the same way Hunter had chuckled at Tab. The unnerving thought that nothing in his world would ever be the same slowly drifted across his mind.

two

Tab glanced at Hunter as he fixed the scrapes on her hands. His hair had slipped forward over his shoulder, the long strands moving to hide his face as he worked. Upon closer inspection, she realized his hair wasn't blond at all. Instead, sun-bleached streaks of gold sifted through layers of darker brown, a testament to the long hours he must spend out of doors. He wore his off-white shirt with the sleeves rolled up to his elbow. His deeply tanned forearms also attested to a large amount of time spent in the great outdoors.

She startled as she realized his brown-eyed gaze now met hers. A grin surrounded by tiny laugh lines filled out his mouth as he watched her perusal.

"Whatd'ya think?" He settled back on his heels, the gauze held loosely in his hand.

"Excuse me? Oh, about the scrapes? I'm sure they'll be fine."

He laughed, and she liked the sound. "I actually referred to your examination of me. Now I feel like one of your specimens. Do I pass muster?"

A flush spread up Tab's face. "I'm sorry. But you were so intent, and I'm curious about a man such as yourself who seems like a loner yet is so kind to someone who hasn't exactly welcomed him with open arms."

The flush deepened at the mental image of her arms open to welcome him into an embrace. "Oh, I don't mean open arms as in a hug or embrace. I only meant. . .oh, never mind."

His deep laugh filled the air again. "I know what you meant. But we're neighbors, and we need to work in close proximity. I feel it's only right for me to help if there's a need."

"Well, we're also competitors, and surely you have that in the back of your mind. I'm sure not everyone would be as gentlemanly as you've been, especially when it comes to an accident-prone female. A female who isn't even welcome in their presence." She shrugged at her own words, trying to put on a brave front. For some reason, she felt it important that she not look pathetic in front of Hunter.

Hunter stared at her for a moment. "I feel peace over the outcome of the event. Whatever happens, whoever finds the first bone, finds the first bone. It's just the way it will be."

"So you don't care about the win and getting your name on the plaque?" Tab could hear the disbelief in her own voice. She crossed her arms and stared him down. Everyone wanted the recognition. "In all my twenty years, that's all my father has lived for. Surely you didn't sign on and come all the way out here not expecting to win."

"Of course not. I fully intend to do my utmost to claim the prize. But I can only do my best and work in the way I've trained. The rest will fall in place as it will."

Hunter glanced across the road at a couple of rough-looking men setting up camp a few spots down from them. Tab had noticed earlier that the two men couldn't even figure out which way their tent went together. They'd bickered loudly from the moment they'd arrived.

He nodded his head in their direction. "I'm more concerned about the untrained treasure seekers who are here, that they'll in some way ruin what we've come to do. Though most of the men around the site—excuse me, and you—seem professional and ready to work with careful precision, I'm afraid some of the novices will destroy any find before it's properly recorded."

He abruptly changed gears and turned on his grin again, his eyes crinkling at the corners. "And I have to admit, when I first saw you arrive with your father, I had the thought that even you didn't belong out here and would only be trouble for those around you."

Tab snorted and quickly threw her hand over her mouth in an attempt to cover up the unladylike sound. "And here I've proven you so wrong!"

Hunter's belly laugh caused some of the men, including her father, to glance their way in surprise.

"Yes. And since you've already proven you're destined to be a nuisance to me, why don't you let me give you a hand and we'll get your camp in order."

He gestured for her to lead the way, and though a smart retort of independence lingered on her tongue, she bit it back and accepted his help. Her father hadn't shaken off his strange mood, and if they were going to have shelter by nightfall, she'd need the assistance Hunter offered.

❧

The next day at lunch, Hunter joined the line of men moving along the food table and accepted his plate from one of the cooks. He'd arrived early, as usual, and had his choice of tables. He chose one that faced his camp, allowing him to watch over his personal area while he ate. Tabitha and her father still hovered over their research.

After a slow morning of going over his notes, Hunter

welcomed the chance to meet some of the other competitors. He'd noticed that Tabitha and her father also spent the morning going over notes and textbooks and hadn't had time for more than a brief wave across the expanse of dirt that separated their camps. Snatches of their conversation had drifted his way as they discussed the climate, weather, work locations, and their setup of camp.

Apparently, they did all their work by the book and used only the most up-to-date scientific procedures to track their progress. They also made meticulous notes of their journey. Though he was intrigued by their devotion, he knew his head would explode if he gave in to such tedious ways.

"Mind if I settle here for a bite of lunch?"

Hunter glanced up at the older man who had staked his claim across from the Augustines to the east. "I'd be happy to have you join me. Have a seat."

The man pulled out the chair opposite Hunter, looking more miner than archaeologist, but Hunter had met all types in this field of work. He studied his lunch companion as he settled in. Worn suspenders held up loose trousers, and his sweat-stained gray shirt had seen better days, but the man wore a kind expression on his face and seemed a kindred spirit.

"Name's Jason Walker." He reached out his hand, appeared to notice the dirt on it, and then shrugged and pulled it back with a sheepish smile. "It's mighty kind of them to provide a cook and the grub so we can focus on our work, don'tcha think?" He tried to tame his wild gray hair with a grimy hand and waited for Hunter's reply.

Hunter, his mouth full, nodded in agreement. He swallowed the surprisingly good food before offering his name.

The man grinned. "Well, Hunter, I can't help but notice that you already seem mighty smitten with our neighboring female."

Hunter choked on the sip of water he'd just taken and glanced around to see if anyone else had heard the comment. After he'd regained his composure, he leveled a look at the older man. "No disrespect intended, Jason, but I'm only trying to be neighborly and lend a hand when needed."

"If I might be so bold—" The man hesitated.

Nothing has stopped you from being outspoken thus far, so why stop now? crossed Hunter's mind. He quickly offered up a prayer for patience and forgiveness for his unkind thoughts and reminded himself that he'd come to lunch hoping to meet some other people.

"Please feel free." As soon as he'd spoken the words, Hunter noticed Tabitha and her father heading his way.

Jason's words carried across the quiet air. "I'd say you've done a mighty fine job of staking your claim on that beauty. She's a looker, that one is—just as pretty as can be. And smart! Why, she could write books with all her knowledge that would rival anything out there, from what I've heard." Jason sent a gap-toothed smile across the table. "Yep, you done did a fine thing in capturing her attention."

Tabitha stopped in her tracks, a look of horrified embarrassment passing across her features. She stared at the two men while her father bumped into her from behind, his dishes sliding dangerously close to his chest. Hunter held his breath in anticipation of a mess, but Dr. Augustine stepped back and righted his tray just in time to prevent anything from spilling. Apparently he was used to his daughter's abrupt stops. Maybe the duo wouldn't realize Jason had referred to Tabitha in his conversation.

"Please, join us." Hunter jumped to his feet and pulled out the chair beside him. Tabitha sent him a look of death and stalked over to place her tray next to his.

"Well, isn't this wonderful!" Jason also stood and offered Tabitha a slight bow. "We've just been talking about you, and here you are. It must be a divine appointment."

So much for her not knowing whom Jason referred to with his flowery talk. Flowery talk at Hunter's expense. And now he couldn't even deny his "claim" on Tabitha without embarrassing the poor woman further.

"A divine appointment? I don't think I understand." Tabitha voiced her confusion after introductions had been made.

"Why, you know, a meeting set up by the Almighty."

Tabitha glanced upward at the sky, following the direction of Jason's upraised finger. "The, um, Almighty?" Her perplexed eyes sought out Hunter's, the question in them asking about Jason's sanity.

"I think he's referring to God." Hunter turned to his new friend. "Am I right?"

"Well, of course you're right. My Lord and Savior. Who else would I be referring to?"

"It's a bunch of nonsense if you ask me." Dr. Augustine sat and grunted down at his meal.

"You're not a believer?" Hunter asked.

"No. And I take it you are?"

"Yes, sir, absolutely."

"Hmm." His single comment showed his disdain.

Though Jason's comment confirmed he was a kindred spirit just as Hunter had thought, he felt sad that Tabitha, or at least her father, would have a hard time understanding and sharing his belief in God. It would figure that with their training and background, they wouldn't hold the same beliefs as him. And as he'd first suspected, also because of their scientific training, they might have a hard time understanding an intangible concept such as faith. He set the revelation aside for prayer.

૨ે

Tab enjoyed the rest of her meal with her neighbors. Though at first they'd made her uncomfortable with their personal talk about her and then with their mention of God and religion, the conversation soon moved on to more pleasant topics, such as the weather and the dig. Her father had become surprisingly talkative during the past half hour.

"I'm just saying there's a lot of danger involved in this type of setting. I think each of us needs to be extra careful and diligent and to watch what's going on around us."

The words made Tabitha focus back on the men's conversation. "Dangerous in what way, Father? I've not sensed anything dangerous around us." Her traitorous eyes chose that moment to dart a glance at Hunter. He grinned. She felt her eyes briefly widen. Surely he couldn't read her thoughts and know the very word *danger* made her think of him! And the danger he represented had nothing to do with anything but a danger to her heart. She shook off the silly notion and shifted around slightly in her chair, the movement placing her back to him, which was ridiculous, because now her back was to her dining companions, and how could she hold an intelligent conversation with the three men while facing away from them and into the empty air?

With a frustrated huff, she turned back to the table, grasped the seat of her chair with both hands, and hopped it over a few inches away from the distracting man. Her father sent her a confused look and frowned. She froze where she was and reached up to twiddle with a strand of hair. "Father, the danger? What is it you're referring to?"

He looked away and refused to meet her gaze. "I mean exactly what I've said. Just be aware of your surroundings and be careful."

"Father, why are you so reticent? It isn't like you."

He ignored her question and continued to eat.

Tabitha looked at Hunter, but he seemed as baffled by her father's words as she felt. Something wasn't right, but she had no clue how to force him to open up to her. She felt adrift and alone and suddenly welcomed the companionship and close proximity of the annoying man in the next chair. With her father's withdrawal, she'd have to rely on Hunter if anything did go wrong. The thought was at once both reassuring and alarming. She bent over her plate and hurried to finish. She'd feel a lot better when she returned to the routine comfort of their newest dig.

three

The idea of gathering for dinner as a group later that evening made Tabitha most uncomfortable. Never one to be at ease in a large group, she felt even more out of her element when women were so scarce at events such as this one. She glanced around. Forget scarce, make that nonexistent. She alone filled the female category. She knew she stood out like a sore thumb and also knew most men actually resented her presence and would hurry to blame her and "bad luck" for any mishap that occurred while she stayed at the dig.

Her father followed her to the flat side of a rock formation where they'd have a good view of their coordinator when he stood to speak and explain the rules. The setting sun lowered into the horizon on the far side of the butte, allowing them a respite from the heat that had lingered over the barren area throughout the day. Though Tab and her father hadn't thought to bring a crate over to sit on, she refused to perch on the dusty rocks and chose instead to stand with arms crossed defensively over her chest for the contest overview.

She found herself glancing around at the others as they arrived—the area bustled with activity and boisterous talk—and assured herself that she wasn't looking for anyone in particular. She only scouted out the competition. But her traitorous heart picked up speed and skipped a few beats when her eyes met those of Hunter as he approached from the path to her right. Since he'd rescued her from the wall of luggage that had buried her the previous day, and then had helped her get their cantankerous tent stakes deep into the hard-packed dirt, and *then* allowed them to join him for that awkward lunch, it was only natural that she'd greet him with a warm smile of recognition. Wasn't it? The others around her were strangers, and her father continued to be distant. Jason was nowhere to be found, and she needed to feel she had a friend.

Her mouth curved into a smirk over her musings. Her mind hadn't drifted far from thoughts of her intriguing neighbor the entire night before, nor for the majority of her recent waking hours today, even with all that had to be done. She'd been aware of Hunter's every move, a fact that didn't slip past her sharp mind, and those moves pretty much drove her to distraction.

Tab couldn't afford to be sidetracked or unfocused. This project held too much importance to her father and his future. With forty-two years behind him, her father was getting older, and she'd seen a certain despondence come over him of late. She'd determined to help him achieve this one important goal before she had to watch him retire to the scholarly world that awaited the end of his travels. Though she knew he'd be a wonderful professor, she also knew a part of him would die when he had to give up this aspect of his career. She'd do whatever she could to keep him going in the meantime. This last award would go a long way in keeping him young and inspired.

"I see you brought your favorite chair." The quip popped out before she thought to stop it.

"Only in case I met a damsel in distress who didn't bring her own. How fortunate for you and your tired feet that I've arrived with my chair in tow and can offer rest for the weary." Hunter had reached her side and now grinned as he spun the hardwood chair around with a flourish and set it at her side.

He wore his hair pulled back and fastened at his neck with a leather band and had donned another off-white shirt that he'd tucked neatly into dark brown slacks. Tabitha felt grungy and dusty by comparison.

Tab's face warmed with embarrassment for the umpteenth time that day as many sets of eyes turned their way and stared. Never had she blushed so much in any man's presence. "I'm fine, thank you. And I don't need to sit." No way would she sit in a proper chair while all the men around her stood or sat on rocks or on the hard-packed dirt that covered the ground. She preferred to blend in.

Hunter stared her down. "Nonsense. I've watched you work all day—and I didn't miss the refusals to my offers of help. Sharing my chair is the least I can do. Now let me be a gentleman and just for once accept the kindness of a neighbor."

She opened her mouth to argue.

He sighed, placed his hands on her shoulders, and eased her into the seat. "Please sit."

She popped back to her feet, her face flaming more than ever. "I beg your pardon! I'll sit if I want, and I'll stand if I prefer, and tonight I feel like—"

"Tabitha, dear, forget the tirade and do as the gentleman says. He has nothing but your best interests at heart." Tabitha's father had to choose this moment to break his silence of the past couple days. He stood with his pipe in hand and stared down at her with forcefulness completely out of character.

Tabitha didn't see how she could refuse the offer now, with

every eye in the place focused their way, without looking petty. She smoothed her skirt over her backside and slid into place on the chair. The relief to her aching feet was immediate, and she momentarily closed her eyes in pleasure. When she opened them, Hunter was watching her.

Always the gentleman, at least in appearance, he tried to hide his smile. "See? That wasn't so bad, was it?"

"It's actually pretty heavenly, I have to admit. But I could have lived without the public spectacle." She scowled up at him before turning her attention on the other men around them. They'd all gone back to their conversations without another thought given to her.

"Then next time be a lady and accept graciously instead of insisting on acting like one of the men."

Tabitha would have shot to her feet to deny his comment, but her father's hand suddenly appeared on her shoulder and held her firmly in place, though he never looked her way. She had to admit Hunter had a point. Her thoughts had strayed to the men around them and her desire to keep on par with them instead of accepting Hunter's offer in good faith.

"I'll keep your advice in mind, though I doubt I'll have opportunity in the future to accept any more of your manly demands." If she thought her face had burned at its hottest level of embarrassment in the previous moments of conversation, she'd been sorely mistaken. That sensation had been a cool breeze compared to the flame of heat that now crossed her features as she realized what she'd just said. The minute the words crossed her lips she wished to call them back, but it was too late. Even her father seemed to be snickering, or else the dust had settled into his lungs in a sudden way that had him grabbing for his handkerchief, which he hurriedly settled over his mouth.

৯

Hunter watched as the coordinator strutted to the makeshift stage.

"Welcome, all, to the Statford Museum's first dinosaur dig. As you all know, this area became known for the dinosaur discoveries that began about thirty years ago." Joey Matthews stood with his heels together, toes pointed outward, and held his jacket by the lapels as he stared out over the audience. "I'm sure you've all received and read the papers I sent outlining the competition, but I feel it's necessary to touch on a few of the more important topics. As you know, Statford Museum is privately owned and located in the state of New York. I'm the on-site coordinator of this event, and all problems and questions need to go through me. We've tried to keep the contest simple and only have a few specific requirements all participants must follow.

"First and foremost, respect the area and the others around you. We'd all like to win the cash prize and the chance for recognition, but let's make sure we only do so by following the rules set before us. You can work alone or in a partnership. Your original papers should be filled out with this information, but if you have a change, please let me know immediately. If you sign on as a partnership, you'll be expected to share the winnings equally. Whatever measures you use, keep the other participants' safety in mind at all times.

"We're looking for the first bone found to signify a dinosaur skeleton. After the find, the bones will be carefully wrapped in tissue paper and dipped in plaster, packed in straw, placed in a sturdy crate, and sent out of here by horse-drawn freight very similar to the wagons that brought most of you out here. Items will then be shipped by railroad to their final destination. We have a doctor available, and we can take trips to Vernal for any of your needs. If you have any questions, I'll be available after this speech."

A thrum of chatter erupted as Joey stepped off the stage. The participants dispersed into small groups and headed back to their tents, a feeling of excitement in the air.

The next morning Hunter had a hard time focusing and settling into a routine with Tabitha's words and charming reactions the night before buzzing through his head. He'd cleared the area for his claim and now worked to set up a rope and stake circumference to enclose the spot he'd chosen. By arriving early, he'd had the pick of the dig site and, through careful analysis, had plotted the best layout.

Though the surrounding outcroppings south of him were also in the dig site, he'd bumped his ropes up against them so no one else could settle in that direction. Tabitha and her father had set up just to the north, and the area to the west was no-man's-land. Thus the rest of the hustle and bustle of activity all happened to the east, allowing them a quiet corner to do their work.

Hunter didn't miss the fact that Tabitha and her father had chosen their dig area just as carefully and with just as much thought. Their tent was placed immediately to the west of their dig site and bumped up against the western cliffs just as he'd bumped his site up against the ones to the south. It made for a cozy and protected setup.

He glanced over and caught Tab watching him. For a woman who had grown up in a man's world, she blushed more than any other female he'd ever met. He found himself wondering about her mother and how she'd come to be her father's sole companion. As she glanced his way once more, he tipped his worn leather hat and laughed aloud as she fumbled the strange utensil in her hand, dropping it to tangle in her long, tan skirt. Her white shirtsleeves were rolled up in the same fashion as his, and he noted that her arms were every bit as tan. He smiled. He liked a woman who didn't cave in to pretentious ways—though the way she and her father traveled, more than likely she didn't even know what convention was.

Tab stood to her feet and hurried his way. His heart jumped in anticipation, a strange occurrence he'd have to dissect and mull over at a later time.

"I'll thank you to please quit staring at me and focus instead on your work." Her hiss was just above a whisper, but the words hit their mark as she'd surely intended. With the sun bearing down, he squinted toward her, trying to figure out if she was serious or teasing.

"I mean it. Every time I look over at you, you're like those paintings where the eyes follow my every move. It's creepy. You have to stop."

Apparently she meant it. He tamped down his amusement as her words made him bristle in anger. Where had their camaraderie of the previous twenty-four hours gone?

He stepped closer. "Then you admit you were staring at me first. Why else would you keep looking over at me? Surely you have enough men at your disposal that you don't have to send simpering glances my way every minute of the day. I have quite enough to keep me busy without you or your glances causing me a distraction."

She gasped and stomped her dainty boot. "Yet you admit

I'm causing you a distraction."

They glowered at each other for a few moments before she spoke again.

"And trust me, I'm truly sorry there aren't more women at your disposal so that you're stuck watching my every move during every waking hour."

With her final comment, she turned and huffed back to her father and their dig. And following suit, he huffed and stalked back to his, muttering all the way about women who didn't know their place and strayed into areas that should belong to men alone. He surprised himself as he silently admitted that he didn't at all regret her being the lone woman at his disposal, for he already knew with her around, no other woman would cause him any distraction at all. He enjoyed watching her every move. The thought completely disconcerted him.

As a diversion to his own traitorous thoughts, he grabbed up his dynamite and decided to shake things up a bit. If his progress went any slower, it would stop completely. The process needed a jump start. The way some of the excavators were working, it would be decades before they ever got close to the bones. And the sooner the first bone was found and the wannabes cleared out of the area, the sooner his thoughts could refocus on his work.

❧

Tab carefully settled in with her back to the infuriating male specimen who just had to choose the spot behind them for his dig. Though the annoying thought did cross her mind that he'd been there first and they were the ones who had made the choice to join him, she pushed it aside and continued on her mental tirade. There were so many other men in the area, and any one of them would have been a fine neighbor, if not downright pleasant to share a work area with. But no, she had to be saddled with a wild card maverick with nothing better to do than ogle her and crowd in on her space. She sat back on her heels to ease her aching muscles, resettled her skirt, and glanced around.

For instance, take that nice old man in the spot directly across the road to their east. Jason. He lifted a hand in greeting, and she waved back. He'd be a fine neighbor, but instead had to be all the way across the dusty road from them. That left them too far away to share pleasantries other than the brief wave he'd just sent her when he'd caught her eye and possibly some more discussion over meals. But when she caught Hunter's eye, he smiled that knowing smile of his, yet she had no idea what exactly it was that he seemed to think he knew!

Then there was the quiet young man across the way and to the north of Jason. That man had yet to look her way, content to do his job and leave others to do theirs. And even the coordinator, ladies' man though he seemed to think he was, gave her a wide berth after their initial meeting the day they'd arrived.

Only Hunter seemed to think it was his self-proclaimed duty either to watch out for her or to drive her insane. With the museum-provided outdoor kitchen area covering both sides of the road to their north, Hunter alone was the closest "neighbor." Oh well, she'd just have to keep her back to him and allow him to work in peace. Hopefully he'd do the same and things could get on from there.

Before resuming the backbreaking task of meticulously scraping the dirt away miniscule piece by miniscule piece, she reached back to resettle her wayward strands of hair. Her hat always fell backward, so she adjusted it forward to better shade her face. The tiniest bone could signify a find, and even fossils led to other discoveries. She made sure her hair stayed out of her face, which allowed her to have complete focus on the area she processed.

Her father worked with the same methodical precision at the far end of their claim, nearest the kitchen area. They'd slowly process each grain of dirt until they met in the middle and would only then move back to their separate sides to begin the same routine one row over. Both had their own sets of equipment, and seldom did they stop to discuss an angle or process or to consult their plans.

Tab couldn't help herself and glanced at Hunter again, her arms midair in fixing her hair back into the braid that slipped from behind her hat. Now there was a man who didn't seem to even know the word *process*, and she had yet to figure out the rhyme or reason behind his routine.

Even now he stalked back and forth, setting new stakes or something into the ground on the bluff side of his claim. How he ever thought he'd find the intricate makings of a dinosaur while pacing about on his feet was beyond her. She shrugged and knelt into place, her knees lining up with the slight indentations made from her previous work. Her long skirt came in handy while providing a bit of cushion for her sore knees. During the next break, she'd pop over to the tent and retrieve the small knee cushion she'd fashioned for a situation such as this.

Digging through her small crate of tools, she decided to use her smallest pick. Tapping delicately at the crusty earth, she bent close to concentrate on the intricate work before her. She reached for a bigger pick and tapped gently with her hammer to break the unrelenting soil. Several taps later, she'd formed a crack. The area rarely received rain, and though mud would be awful to work in, a bit more forgiving earth would certainly make the tedious job easier. Tipping a chisel in the other direction, she grinned as she levered a large chunk of dirt up, allowing her to peer into a small hole. She placed the chunk into a shallow pan beside her. After finishing with the hole, she'd go through the large piece of dirt before dropping the softened mass back into place and moving on.

She now leaned down on her side, carefully excavating the hole to make it bigger. Disappointment set in. Though she knew they'd be here for weeks, every moment created hope that the next move would find the elusive bone they all strove for. At any minute, even this early in the dig, the cry could come around that the competition was over before it had hardly started, so the stress to make that find constantly kept her on edge.

Tabitha gathered her shaky nerves and leaned closer for a better look. A large magnifying glass helped her see there was indeed. . .nothing to see. With a sigh, she picked up her small pick and leaned in for more digging. Something white nestled at the farthest corner, and she worked to get it loose. The moment took her utmost concentration.

A huge booming explosion rocked the area around them with a repercussion that threw Tabitha forward several inches. Gasping for breath, her heart about to beat out of her chest, she and her father scrambled to their feet while others around them glanced their way before returning to work with shakes of their heads.

"Father, whatever was that? Why are we the only ones who seem alarmed?"

She turned to look at her father, but his attention had settled on Hunter and his claim. She followed his gaze and saw that the man in question stood with his hands on his hips and stared at the wall of sandstone before him.

"Confounded young'uns," her father muttered before walking off in the direction of the outhouse.

Tabitha remembered the "stakes" she thought Hunter had been setting out. Realization overcame her, and before she knew it, she'd stalked his way, stepped over his rope divider, and now stood mere inches away from the crazy man. "Dynamite? You used *dynamite* to clear the rock away from your work area? Are you insane?" She'd heard and read about the maverick methods some men used to clear an area to access deeper locations, but never had she seen it in action until now.

Hunter turned and greeted her with his disarming grin, motioning toward the rock. "What d'ya think? I've watched you itching the ground over there for most of the day to get inches into your work area, and in one blast I just 'dug' six feet into the wall of stone here."

"And you probably 'blew up' six feet worth of relics and artifacts, you big baboon! Any fragment of dinosaur skeleton that was near the surface of the earth has surely just been blown to pieces." Tabitha couldn't even stand in one place, she felt so angry and restless. "Why would you take such a chance and risk ruining history in this way?"

Much to her humiliation, tears formed in her eyes. This was their livelihood, and she truly loved her history. It broke her heart to see the callousness of some of the people in their "field."

"Aw, Tabitha, don't cry. I didn't mean to upset you. Look over here a minute. If I were to pick away at this wall of rock, I'd never get six inches in before the end of the competition. The bones aren't going to be lying on top of the ground waiting for us. We have to dig deep."

"So you throw history to the wind and take the chance of ruining something all for greed?"

He stared at her for a moment in silence. "No. I'm not indiscriminate. If you'll look closer, you'll see which type of rock this is. Have you ever heard of bones being found in such?"

He'd caught her off guard. She stepped toward him and did as he asked. He towered over her, and his nearness interfered with her concentration, but she had to admit he had a point. The blasts had only removed the outer rock that hid the more important area within. Now that she focused more intently, she saw he'd used precision skill to achieve such a feat without endangering the precious rock centimeters away from the blast.

"You're experienced with this."

"Of course. I wouldn't risk anyone's safety. I spent years working with my grandfather in his mining business. I used a very small amount of explosive. I'm sorry the repercussion caught you off guard. I'll warn you next time." He grinned. "*If* there is a next time."

"I appreciate it."

The man seemed to have just as special a touch with the way he handled his explosives as the way he expertly handled explosive women.

Such as her.

four

A week had passed with no one claiming a find of any worth. The sun continued its fiery assault on the excavators, causing tempers to flare. More than once Tabitha watched as men gave in to the pressure of stress and heat and allowed themselves to be drawn into a brawl. Several of the confrontations were between the two scraggly men a couple spots down. Each time she noticed Hunter would move into the roadway that ran between the men's site and theirs, and he would either intervene to stop the feud or, if other men beat him to it, he'd stand nearby as if watching over her and her father.

Her father, for the most part, ignored all that went on around them and continued with his work. She still hadn't broken through his self-imposed isolation, nor had she figured out what was causing it. So instead, she focused on furthering her detailed work—far away from Hunter's side of the line. She kept her back to him as much as possible to enhance her concentration, but at meals she found herself drawn to him and settled in to eat with the only friend she'd made.

"I take it your father is working through lunch again?" Hunter stood and held her chair as she sat.

They'd taken to eating at the table nearest their claims, while the other contestants filled the surrounding tables and left them on their own. At first, Tabitha felt uncomfortable eating alone with Hunter, but the few times he wasn't there, she'd felt even worse dining by herself. And once, when she'd avoided his table in the hopes that Jason or some of the other men would join him in case she scared them off, she noticed he'd dined alone anyway. After calling her on her action, he'd insisted she not worry about the others and dine with him.

"Yes, he's skipping another meal, and I'm worried about him." She glanced over to where her father continued his work under the hot sun with no break.

"Is it determination to find a bone? Is he always like this?" Compassion shone through Hunter's eyes, and she knew he really cared.

"Not usually. He's never been this determined or stand-offish. His whole temperament is different here. In a way, I wish I could just pack us up and leave, but the competition's too important to both of us, and we'd be sorry later."

Hunter nodded and pushed back his empty tray. "Would it help if I talked to him?"

Tabitha felt the first smile of the day slip across her lips. "If he won't talk or listen to me, I highly doubt he'll give you the time of day."

His look of disappointment made her feel bad.

"It's nothing personal against you, but he's partial to me and hasn't ever been this way before. I highly doubt you, as a stranger, can break through his wall." She sent him a teasing grin. "Dynamite won't even work in this case."

"You're never going to let me live that down, are you?" He captured her hand in his, catching her off guard. "I said I'd not resort to that process again, though you have to admit the technique was well done and pretty amazing."

"Right, and said with such humility." She rolled her eyes.

"I still have a bruise on my shoulder from the repercussion knocking me forward. I'm not sure that's a sign of total proficiency and excellence."

Hunter's cockiness vanished immediately. "Why didn't you say something before? I'm so sorry. I didn't have any idea you'd be affected, or I'd have never done it."

Tabitha felt bad that she'd brought it up. "No harm done. Forget it." She pushed her tray away, too, and stood, sending him what she hoped was a cheery smile. "We'd best be getting back."

"Tab."

She froze midstep and turned back to him.

"How can I forget it? I really am sorry. I don't want you brushing this off. You should have told me before that I'd hurt you. That's the last thing I'd ever want to do."

She reached over and tugged at his hand. "I know, and I accept your apology. Now, c'mon. To show that your apology is fully accepted, I'll let you walk me back to my site."

Hunter stared at her a moment, his face a mask of surprise. "I must say, that's a huge step for you! Are you sure you don't mind?" He glanced around covertly. "Someone might see us and realize you are, in fact, a girl."

To her surprise he hadn't released her hand, so she let go of his instead and gave him a mock punch on the arm. "No, I don't mind."

He swung into step with her. "Will your father faint with shock?"

Tabitha laughed at his antics. She'd never met a man as playful and fun as Hunter before. Her colleagues were always like her father, serious and busy. And they all made an effort to ignore her, or worse, pretended she didn't exist. "He'll probably thank you. I think you're his break from me, and since he doesn't seem too big on my company these days, I know I appreciate your companionship and caring."

Embarrassed, she heard the note of sadness that carried over into her words. "I'd better get to work. I have to run over to my tent for a moment before getting busy again."

Hunter searched her eyes for a moment and nodded. "I'll see you at dinner, then. Save me a spot if you get there first."

The last was said in jest, because they both knew Hunter was the early bird, while she and her father seemed to run late at every turn.

Tabitha fluttered her hand at him and stepped over the low-set rope that surrounded their work site. She entered the tent, and the captured humidity sucked her breath away. The area, with only enough space for two cots and each of their trunks of clothing along with a few crates of supplies, was closed off from any breeze and at least ten degrees hotter than the air outside. She hurried to grab the book she needed before heading back outside.

Just as she reached the opening, something hard landed on the end of the tent where she'd stood moments earlier, crushing the back corner to the ground. She screamed and heard footsteps running from outside.

"Tab!"

Hunter's worried voice echoed her father's as both men reached the flap. Tabitha heard them behind her but remained frozen in place, looking at the damage to the interior of the tent. A large tear in the fabric exposed the back corner to the elements. The stake had been ripped from the ground. Her cot lay at her feet, now a splintered mess.

After realizing she was fine, Hunter hurried outside and

around the back corner as her pale father led her in his wake. She could hear Hunter's loud words of anger.

They rounded the tent and saw him standing, hands on hips, glaring up at the cliff behind their camp.

"What's going on over here?" Joey Matthews pushed his way through the crowd that had gathered and hurried over to where they stood. "What's causing this interruption to everyone's day?" He glared at Tabitha, as if her very presence drew everyone over.

Hunter spun and glared back at Joey. "What's 'causing this interruption' is a very large boulder that was pushed off the cliff and onto the Augustines' tent while Tabitha was inside."

"Pushed? Now, c'mon, who'd want to do something like that and why? Maybe you ought to keep the accusations down." Joey's face turned red with anger. "I run a clean contest, and I don't like the insinuation that something malicious would happen on my watch."

"Well, then you explain to me how something like this could randomly happen and just as Tabitha happened to enter her tent?"

Joey surveyed the scene. "Well, it's quite possible the boulder just came loose and fell. You did put your tents rather close to a cliff, and surely you must have known something like this could happen."

"If rocks such as this formed the butte, then yes, I'd say you had a plausible theory, but if you'll look closer, this rock isn't anything like the formation behind us. This had to have been brought in and pushed. Someone intentionally planned to hurt Tabitha, or her father, in the process. I demand a full investigation."

Joey swept his hat from his head and pushed his hair away

from his eyes before slapping it back in place. "As I said, I run this contest. I can choose who stays and who goes. I'll thank you to remember that. And I'd appreciate your not telling me how to do my job. I'll investigate if and when I feel there's a valid reason." He turned and stalked back toward the crowd.

The men surrounding them didn't budge. Joey faced them. The men began one by one to cross their arms over their chests, fierce looks of protective anger on their features.

"Surely you all don't agree? Especially those who came to me early on and demanded I send Miss Augustine packing?"

Still no one budged.

"Oh, fine. If you all insist I investigate this ridiculous accusation, I'll do so."

Jason stepped forward and stood toe-to-toe with Joey. "Miss Augustine ain't been anything but a hard worker and one of the men—excuse me, ma'am." He nodded Tabitha's way. He returned to his spiel toward Joey. "So you have no reason to speak to her in this way or to ignore Hunter's request."

"Demand is more like it," Joey muttered. "I said I'll look into it. Now clear out and be on your way."

The men stood a few moments longer, staring Joey down, and then turned as one and headed off in the other direction.

৵

Hunter hurried to Tabitha's side. "Are you sure you're okay?"

Tabitha nodded. "I'd just walked away from there. If I'd dallied or waited a moment longer. . ."

A shudder shook her body. Hunter led her to a nearby crate and eased her down on it. He knew how shook up she was, because she didn't argue or give him a fight. He squatted down to face her. "Do you know anyone here from previous digs? Is there someone you've come across before who might have a grudge or a reason to hurt you?"

Tabitha looked at him, her blue eyes reflecting his worry. "No one. I've never met anyone here before. My father and I work mostly abroad. We've not been in the country for a couple of years until now."

Peter Augustine stood with his back to them, staring at the massive boulder. Now he turned and addressed them. "We'll be pulling out first thing in the morning. Tabitha, I want you packed up and ready to go. This isn't worth the danger. You could have been killed."

"No, Father!" Tabitha jumped to her feet and hurried to his side. "You can't mean it. I bet Mr. Matthews is right and this was a fluke. We can't give up so early in the competition."

Her father stared past her and met Hunter's gaze. "You know as well as I do that this wasn't an accident. Tell her, Mr. Pierce."

Hunter hated to go against her, but her father had a point. "He's right, Tab. This was no accident. And since we don't know why someone would do such a thing, there's no reason to take a chance on your well-being. You need to do as he says and go."

The words lanced his heart, and his pain reflected the expression in Tabitha's eyes as she surveyed him as if he were a traitor. With a sad shake of her head, she turned to go, stalking away from him and out of sight around the front corner of her tent.

"Sir." Hunter wasn't sure what to say, but when he saw the look on Dr. Augustine's face, he felt he had to push forward. "If you want to stay, I promise to help watch over Tabitha. Maybe if we're both on guard. Whoever stood on that butte should have been in plain sight. We just didn't know to look.

Now we do know, so we can. . ."

Dr. Augustine already shook his head. His color hadn't yet returned, and he looked like a ghost. "Son, I appreciate the offer, but I'm going to have to say no." He opened his mouth to say more but froze, a strange expression filling his features.

"I don't feel so. . ." He began to sway and, with a hand reached out toward Hunter, collapsed.

Hunter caught him and called for Tabitha, who rounded the tent in moments.

"Nooo!" Her cry again had men running from all directions. Hunter heard someone call for the doctor to be summoned as he lowered Dr. Augustine's inert form to the ground. Tabitha hurried back into the tent for a blanket, which they folded under her father's head.

"What happened?" her voice shook, and Hunter prayed she'd not faint. They had enough going on.

"I'm not sure. One minute we were talking, and the next he passed out and fell."

The doctor pushed through the crowd, with Joey on his heels. He sent them a glare that implied they'd done this just to ruin his day.

"I've had enough of you people and your theatrics," he growled.

Hunter was on his feet and had the man by the front of his shirt before the words were completely out. "We people didn't ask for any of this. Someone pushed a boulder down on Miss Augustine, and the intent wasn't to scare her. She could have been killed. The aftereffect caused her father to pass out, whether from a weak heart or shock, I don't know. But *your* operation is causing a safety risk, and I think you'd better focus on finding out who's behind it and why, instead of throwing out inappropriate comments."

He shoved the man away and wished the men behind would have let him fall to the ground. Instead, they reached out to steady Joey, who glared more intensely at Hunter as he righted his clothing. But before Hunter's conscience could prick at him for the unkind thought, Jason stepped forward and intervened.

"Mr. Matthews, I have to agree with Mr. Pierce. This ruckus isn't any of these folks' fault, and I don't think you can find a man here who disagrees." He turned to the others. "Am I right?"

The men voiced their agreement.

"You need to stop meddling with these folks and figure out what's going on. If I'm recalling correctly, they aren't the first people to have a situation occur. We've lost five other teams to accidents that sent them scurrying out of the competition. Someone is determined to chase everyone off, and as the head of operations, you need to be finding out who it is and why."

Hunter hadn't realized others left due to mischief or danger, though he did know a few other groups had pulled out. He assumed they decided they weren't cut out for this type of work. It gave him a new appreciation for Tabitha and her perseverance.

He returned his attention to Dr. Augustine and Tabitha. She stood forlornly at the side of the tent while the doctor did his exam. Hunter could hear Jason shooing the other men out of the way.

"He's going to be okay," Hunter whispered to Tabitha. He wrapped a comforting arm around her and pulled her close. She looked as if she'd join her father on the ground at the slightest breeze. She surprised him by relaxing into his support.

The doctor finished his exam and glanced up at them. "Your father's going to be fine, miss. But I'd like to send him in to Vernal for observation. Has he been eating and drinking enough in this heat?"

Tabitha shook her head. "I've tried to get him to eat consistently, but he's skipped several meals. He hasn't been drinking much, either."

"I'll take him back with me, and we'll have him up and on his feet in no time." He stood and dusted off his pants. "My wife and I live nearby, and she'll take good care of him while I'm here during the day. Don't you worry about a thing."

æ

Tabitha watched him go before turning to address Hunter. "How can I not worry? I have no one to stay with. The doc didn't offer me a chance to go along. Should I insist on going with them?"

Hunter thought a moment. "They might not have room for you. I think he'd have offered otherwise. As to what you should do, I think you should sit tight and continue on. We'll be extra diligent, and I'll watch out for you."

Though Tabitha was stressed beyond reason over her father's health, she felt a small jolt of excitement at the thought that Hunter wanted to keep her nearby. But then she reminded herself that he probably felt responsible as her closest friend at the dig and did so out of duty.

"Unless, is there somewhere you could go? Someone you could stay with until your father is well again? Perhaps you could go home to your mother or someone else in your family?"

Then again, maybe he only felt obligated and trapped into watching out for her. A chill passed through her.

"My father's all the family I have. My mother died when I was a toddler, and there's no one else." She kept her voice cool and distanced herself from him. "But don't you worry. I'll be fine on my own. I don't need to burden you with my problems."

Realization quickly replaced the confusion on Hunter's features. "You aren't a burden to me. I'd not have offered my assistance if I hadn't wanted to. Haven't we become friends over the past week?" He tipped her chin up and forced her to look at him. "I'm only thinking of your safety."

"I like to think we've become friends. But really, I am perfectly capable of caring for myself. I've done it many times before."

"Well, not this time. Now you have me."

A warm feeling of contentment swept away the chill, and for the first time in a long time, Tabitha felt she had someone else on her side. She sent Hunter a thankful smile and knelt down next to her father.

"I don't know if you can hear me, Papa, but the doctor's going to take good care of you." She'd reverted out of worry to her childhood name for her father. "I'm going to stay here and continue on, but Hunter has assured me he'll watch out for me. So you have no need to be concerned and can just focus on getting well."

She let her voice trail off as she stared into her father's nonresponsive face. A sob caught in her throat as the doctor pulled up in a wagon. She felt Hunter's strong hands on her shoulder, urging her to her feet.

"He's going to be fine, Tabitha. Look, his color's returning and his breathing is steady."

Hunter was right. She stepped back and allowed the doctor, Hunter, and several other men to lift her unconscious father onto the makeshift bed in the doctor's wagon.

"I'll stay with him for the rest of the day and will bring a report on his condition sometime tomorrow." Doc climbed up onto the seat and took the reins. "If anyone else needs my assistance, send for me."

Hunter nodded, and the horses and wagon carrying her father moved out of sight.

By now the sun was low over the buttes, and Tabitha knew there wasn't time to return to work. They'd had a late lunch and, with all the action, had lost the entire afternoon.

"I'm sorry to have kept you from your work. I'm confirming every superstition all the men have about women on a dig site. I'll bet I've been more of a pain than you'd ever imagined I'd be when you first saw me."

"Well, possibly," Hunter teased. "More entertainment than I'd ever imagined, too. Let's head over and snag a table early, and I'll get you a drink while we wait for dinner."

She let him lead her to the tables grouped near the kitchen.

After he'd brought them mugs of water, he settled in beside her. "So, tell me about your childhood. You lost your mother at a young age, but surely your father didn't set out with a toddler in tow while traveling the world."

Tabitha smiled at the picture the comment invoked. "Not quite. We stayed in Boston with my grandmother, my father's mother, for the first few years. Only after I'd become fairly independent did he decide it was time to move on. You'd have liked my granny. She shared similar beliefs with you."

She watched as Hunter's face lit up at the thought. "Your grandmother was a believer? She said she loved the Lord, too?"

Tabitha nodded. "Very much. Not a night went by that she didn't tell me a story from the Bible before bed. I used to find them fascinating."

"And your father was okay with that?"

"My father had no choice in the matter. My granny loved the Lord, and she ran a tight ship. No one dared to cross her, not even my father. He was one of seven sons. Granny was the tiniest little thing, but she stood her ground. My father was the only one of her sons who refused to embrace her beliefs. Even in later years, when my papa tried to dissuade her from her teachings, she'd set him straight. She always told him he'd regret choosing his belief in evolution over her belief in creation."

"So he's heard the truth, too."

"He's heard her version of the truth. It doesn't necessarily mean it's the truth."

Hunter's face dimmed as he listened to her choice of words. "So you don't believe your granny's way to be the truth?" His earnest expression led her to believe her next few words would make a huge impact on their friendship. She didn't want to let him down but couldn't lie to him, either.

"I'm not completely sold on the theory of evolution."

"So you're open to hearing other thoughts and ideas? Have you studied the Bible or searched for the truth yourself? I can help you if you'd like."

He reached over and took hold of her hand again.

"And your 'help'—it would be completely unbiased, right?" She softened her sarcastic retort with a small smile.

"Well, maybe not entirely. But your grandmother had a

few short years, while your father has had—what—well over
a decade since to give you his point of view on the subject?"
His devotion to the topic was endearing. "I'm just saying that
while you're waiting for him to recuperate, you might want to
delve into the subject a bit more deeply on your own. . .with
my help." His eyes twinkled over his words. "I'll loan you my
Bible. Please?"

She hesitated.

"For me?"

Still she hesitated.

"For your grandmother then. . ."

Now he'd stopped playing fair. She'd adored her grandmother and missed her dearly. Only the small hope in the
back of her mind that her granny had indeed been right and
now sat in her beloved Lord's presence helped take away the
grief when the older woman died. That fact was something
Tabitha had never admitted or verbalized to her father, but
she suddenly found herself wanting to share with Hunter.

"I promise to keep an open mind."

"Good, then let me start by praying with you for your
father."

Hunter clutched her hand tightly in his own. A peace and
contentment descended over her that had nothing to do with
his reverent words or kindness.

five

The next morning Hunter slapped his hand against Tabitha's tent and called out for her to wake up.

"What time is it?" Tabitha's voice sounded husky from sleep, and he tried to envision what she looked like at this early hour. As groggy as she sounded, he might not find out for quite a while.

"It's time for you to be up and about. We have a lot to do today."

"I thought today was Sunday, our mandatory day of rest."

Hunter heard her rustling around inside the tent. He knew the long hours of the required day off would allow her more time to worry about her father, so he figured this would be a good chance to take her to see some of the sights in the surrounding area.

A melancholy sigh drifted out to him. "I can't believe the night has already ended. I tossed and turned, every noise alerting me to the fact that someone might be lurking outside my tent. And I worried about my father. Without him snoring away in the cot beside mine, I felt alone and vulnerable. I didn't realize how much I'd come to rely on him. He's always been there for me."

Hunter knew she'd moved onto her father's cot to sleep, since the damage to her own made it unusable. He'd taken her cot back to his camp the night before so he could rebuild it before Dr. Augustine returned. While he'd worked on the cot, Tabitha had sewn the rip in the tent, doing most of the stitching by lantern late into the night.

"I've borrowed two horses. I have something I want you to see. The excursion will only take up the morning. After we return for lunch, if Doc hasn't returned with an update, we'll ride into town and check on your father."

Tabitha finally appeared through the opening of the tent and stepped out into the early morning sunlight. A pink ribbon wound through her long blond braid and neatly formed a bow at the end. Though dark circles ringed her eyes and proved her lack of sleep, she looked pretty in a dainty floral blouse and flowing pink skirt. Since he'd only seen her in work clothes up until now, the change in her appearance took his breath away.

"You look wonderful." He'd stopped himself short of saying beautiful, not wanting to scare her off.

The color his remark put into her cheeks matched the outfit she wore and made her eyes appear even bluer, a perfect match to the blue of the early morning sky above.

"So, what do you think of my plans?" He pointed toward the two mounts that waited on the road.

"I like them, but could we switch things around and go to see my father first? I'd really like to check on him."

Hunter shook his head. "Doc said he'd stop by with a report. I don't think we should bother them until then. He would have sent for you if things looked worse during the night. Let him do his job. I bet he'll be back here before we return."

"I suppose." Tabitha led the way toward the breakfast table, her dainty boots leaving small imprints in the dust.

Hunter hadn't realized how petite she was, but now, without her work gear on, she seemed to have diminished in size. Or maybe the change reflected her insecurity with her father gone.

They ate quickly in the mostly empty kitchen area and set out on their trek. Hunter led the way, explaining about the different plants and rocks as they rode. Though Tabitha freely admitted her worry about her father, she also admitted this was a most welcome diversion from her sordid thoughts. If he'd left it to her, she'd have sat around and sulked about her father. He was glad he'd thought to busy her with sightseeing.

The day promised to be a beauty and remained cool at this early hour, a fact that Hunter had taken into consideration when planning their itinerary.

He slowed his horse and waited for Tab to come alongside him. He matched her pace as the trail widened. "Other than the obvious, was there a reason for your lack of sleep? Did you hear anyone near your tent during the night?"

"No. My imagination took over from the events of the day. I kept waiting for another rock to crash down on me or for someone to try another approach with my father gone." She rode in silence for a few minutes. "I looked over first thing, used to seeing him nearby on his cot, and it took a moment before I realized he'd fallen ill and wasn't there. The realization brought with it a most awful feeling."

"I'm sorry you're having such a hard time." He paused and thought about her comment. "How about I leave my tent flap open tonight? That might help you feel better."

Tabitha, amused, shook her head. "You'll have a bed full of lizards and other unwelcome critters if you do that. I'm sure I'll be fine. But I appreciate the offer."

"I've been in the area for a while. Usually I don't even bother with the tent. So a few critters aren't going to bother me."

Considering the matter settled, he pulled ahead.

&

Tabitha enjoyed watching him. Today he wore soft brown leather pants and a loose shirt that he didn't bother to tuck into his waistband. The ensemble didn't even remotely resemble the khaki pants and shirt he usually wore. His hair blew free in the breeze, and he looked completely at ease in the saddle. The overall effect gave the impression of a very savage man, one used to riding the trails. If she didn't know him better and had just run into him on the path, he would have terrified her. As it was, she knew he was kind, and his true personality was nothing like the rough image he presented. The thought made her realize she knew nothing about his past or his family, though he already knew most everything there was to know about hers. She determined to use their time together to learn more.

They rounded a large formation of sandstone, and Tabitha's audible gasp caused Hunter to turn in his saddle with a chuckle. "I thought you'd like it."

A valley opened before them, and at the bottom a beautiful winding river carved out a swath in the pink and orange landscape. The array of color against the vivid blue sky took her breath away.

"This alone is worth the ride. The beauty. . .it's like nothing I've seen before. I have no words to describe it." She fell silent.

"Yes, the beauty is without equal."

Hunter's voice sounded reverent, but when she turned to look at him, he stared at her, not the scene before them. The realization flustered her, and she began to chatter, a nervous habit. "If only I could capture the magnificence of this vision to share with my father."

"We'll bring him back as soon as he's up to it. He should be on his feet within a couple of days, and he, too, will have to take a break next week. We'll drag him out here for his own good."

"He'll love it."

"Come on. I have something else to show you."

She followed him, staying close as the trail narrowed.

"Are we safe? I've heard that Butch Cassidy and his gang ride through the area regularly." The hair stood up on the back of her neck as she belatedly remembered that little tidbit of information.

"We should be fine."

"Should be? Or will be?" she teased. For whatever reason, she felt completely safe in Hunter's care. If he wasn't worried, and she felt sure he'd never have brought her here if he had any thoughts of running into an unsafe situation, she wouldn't worry, either. Though she had to admit, the fact that he carried weapons helped her sense of security.

"I promise, while you're in my care, I'll do everything in my power to keep you safe."

She knew he meant it.

They rounded a cliff and Hunter swung down from his saddle before reaching up to assist her. His hands were strong on her waist, and she felt their warmth through the thin fabric of her skirt. He set her before him and held her a moment longer than necessary.

"Have you ever seen petroglyphs before? Or pictographs?"

Tabitha's heart picked up speed in anticipation of what Hunter was about to show her. Or maybe her struggle for air came from his close proximity only a moment before. More than likely, the effect came from a combination of both. "I've seen petroglyphs, but only pictures of them in some of our books."

He led her around the bend and pointed to the canyon wall. She caught her breath in surprise. "Oh, look at all of them! I can't believe there are so many carvings in the wall. It's amazing!"

She ran from one set of inscriptions to the next. "And look over there! Pictographs! They're fantastic. My father will never believe this. He's wanted to see them his whole life, but we didn't realize they were right here where we'd be spending our time. I thought they were farther north."

"My grandfather and I discovered this batch when we were exploring a few months back. I'm writing an article for publication, but as far as I know, nobody else knows of this specific location. The petroglyphs are all through the area." Hunter just stood and grinned at her enthusiasm. "So I guess you're glad I dragged you out here?"

She belatedly remembered her manners and hurried back to him. "Oh, Hunter, yes, thank you! Thank you so much for thinking to bring me here." She threw her arms around him and gave him an exuberant hug. He took a step backward from the force of her hug before grabbing her waist to momentarily stabilize her. Once he'd let go, she hurried back to the walls, trying to figure out what each of the carvings and pictures represented. She turned to him and caught a strange expression on his face. "Are you okay?"

Maybe she'd hurt him, or maybe he just didn't like someone invading his space in that way. Now that she thought about it, she'd been horribly forward. "I'm sorry."

"Why are you apologizing?" He snapped out of his funk

and came to join her in front of the nearest etching.

"You had a funny look on your face. I thought I might have hurt you."

He sent her his charming smile. "You couldn't hurt me if you tried."

❧

As they rode back toward camp, Hunter inwardly laughed at himself. Famous last words. When she'd thrown her arms around him with such abandon, he'd enjoyed it. And he'd felt bereft when she'd pulled away. He'd meant what he'd said, that a petite person like her would never hurt him in the way she'd meant, by hugging him too hard. But for the first time ever, he realized his heart had become entangled with hers, and he'd enjoyed her brief hug far too much. All his life, after watching the family he grew up with and their self-centered ways, he'd been careful to guard his emotions and not let any woman get too close. Yet here, in just over a week, Tab had somehow slipped past his barrier and snagged a bit of his heart. He hadn't even realized, or at least he hadn't admitted it to himself, until that moment.

He'd noticed her beauty right from the start, but after she'd come at him like a wildcat that first day, he'd planned to keep his distance. For whatever reason, that distance had been breached, and here he stood, alone, in the middle of nowhere, with a very dangerous woman. One who was dangerous to him, his bachelorhood, and his future. And more important, he had a feeling she'd prove dangerous to his heart.

He'd have to keep her at arm's length, a task that would be hard with her father ill and no one else to watch over her. He'd given his word and would do his part for now, but as soon as Dr. Augustine returned and took over again as guardian for his daughter, Hunter would return his focus to the find. Tabitha's words broke into his thoughts.

"Hunter? You've been distant and silent the entire ride back. I must have hurt you in some way. Or perhaps it was my forwardness." A look of realization passed through her eyes, and she raised a delicate—and smudged—hand to her mouth. "Oh my, as I'm sure you've noticed, I'm not very wise or experienced in the ways of propriety while under the care of a gentleman, and I do believe I overstepped my bounds."

Her innocence and the way she verbalized her thoughts was refreshing. He couldn't help but smile. The women he'd grown up with would be more shocked about her voicing those very words than they would have been over the spontaneous hug, though the hug would surely have set their tongues a waggin', too.

"You did nothing of the sort. I enjoyed our time together immensely. I'm ecstatic that you found such joy in the sights I took you to see."

He didn't miss the immediate release of her breath or the relief in her light blue eyes. "Oh, good. And we'll still take my father out there next week? It would mean so much to him. To us both."

Hunter hesitated, but only for a moment. "Of course. If he's up to the trip by then, we'll ride out first thing Sunday morning."

Mentally he called himself a coward. Hadn't he just told himself that when her father returned, he'd pull a safe distance away? Then why did he find himself blurting out the surest thing that would put a smile back on her face, without any thought to his decision? Keeping his distance from her would definitely prove to be one of the harder parts of this dig.

They entered camp to see Joey hurrying their way. "You two, over here, right now."

Hunter felt like a wayward schoolboy who'd just been caught sneaking out of class for a day of fishing at the pond. Not that he'd done such a thing in his youth. Well, maybe once or twice. A grin from memories past curved his lip.

"You find something to be amusing?" Joey motioned for them to dismount.

Hunter did as he asked and hurried to assist Tabitha before Joey could get his slimy hands on her. The effort earned him a scowl from the coordinator. "Nope, I find nothing amusing here. But I did just return from a most enjoyable ride and sightseeing excursion with Miss Augustine. That's enough to put a smile on any man's face."

The comment earned him a glare from Joey and a stomp on the foot from Tabitha. A hard stomp. For such a little thing she used the heels of her boots very thoroughly. "Ow!" His teacher's raps against his knuckles paled in comparison.

Joey stalked away and picked up a bundle of papers. "If you can try to focus on the matter at hand..."

Hunter suddenly had a bad feeling about where this conversation would lead. He glanced at Tabitha, and she shrugged. "What's going on?"

"With Miss Augustine's father out of the picture, I must insist she leave the site and return home. A woman without a chaperone at an event such as this is most inappropriate, as you've both just demonstrated." He sent them each a piercing glare. "Didn't you realize how unscrupulous taking off for parts unknown would look?"

Hunter couldn't say he had. One glance at the stricken expression on Tab's face had him pretty sure she hadn't either.

"Tab, I'm sorry. I didn't mean to bring your reputation into question. I should have known better."

She waved away his words, her hand fluttering through the air. "No, I'm sure any thoughts about propriety should have been mine. My instructors at finishing school—before I got kicked out anyway—were very adamant on the weakness of the male species when it came to things of such a nature as this."

Joey stood speechless before them, his mouth gaping open at her comment.

Hunter began to pace, his nervous energy never allowing him to stay still for long. "No, I promised your father I'd look after you and didn't even think about how it would look to ride off alone in such a way. I truly am sorry."

She nodded her acceptance but wouldn't look him in the eye.

"In any case, Miss Augustine, I'm forced to ask you to leave. Surely you agree that it isn't proper for a woman such as yourself to remain here without the guardianship of your father. Your self-appointed guardian has made it clear he isn't up to the task."

Hunter wanted to take Joey to task for the way he'd just publicly embarrassed Tabitha. "We did nothing to harm Miss Augustine's reputation, Mr. Matthews. I'd appreciate your not insinuating anything of the sort. You're embarrassing us both."

Joey's expression became smug. "Perhaps you're embarrassing yourselves. I certainly didn't send you off alone to cause speculation amongst the men."

Hunter made a point of looking around the camp where the other competitors all went about their business, none of them paying the trio any mind at all. "The speculation seems to be all yours." He mimicked Joey's tone of voice. "Perhaps that's because you're the only one in the camp who's curious about our day?"

The man sputtered and ignored Hunter's comment. "As I said, Miss Augustine, you need to pack and leave immediately."

"What's she going to do, Matthews? Walk to the nearest train station and buy a ticket out?" He waved in the direction of the nearest town. "Or do you expect her to put all their belongings on her back and hike out? Be reasonable."

Joey huffed out a frustrated breath. "Of course I don't expect her to do those things. But I do expect her to be ready so that when the next wagon comes through, she'll be able to pull out."

Hunter decided to take a different tack. Tabitha stood in shocked silence as the men debated. He wanted to fix this for her. "Has Doc returned with an update on her father?"

"He arrived earlier this morning, not that you were around to greet him."

"Skip the *theatrics* as you call them, Matthews, and get to the point." Hunter had tired of dancing around with proprieties. He took a menacing step closer to the other man, closing the space between them.

Joey backed away from him and again focused on Tabitha. "I—I, well, he said your father would be fine, and he'd be able to return to work in the next couple of days."

"And yet you threaten Tabitha and tell her you're sending her away. Your actions are despicable, Joey, and you can be sure the people back East who are funding the dig will hear about this." He sent the man a final glare before turning and taking Tabitha by the arm. "Come, Tab. Let's get you back to camp."

As they walked away, he glanced over his shoulder. "Please

make sure the horses are properly cared for."

Joey's face filled with rage. "I'm not here to do your bidding, Pierce. I'll have you remember I'm in charge of this operation."

Hunter stopped and turned around to face him. "Oh, really? I seem to remember you greeting each of us with the comment that we're to come to you if we need anything. And for now, I need you to look after the horses. You've upset Tabitha, and I need to return her to her quarters."

Without another backward glance, he led Tabitha away.

"Do you think he's the one behind the accidents?" Tabitha finally broke her silence when they were a safe distance from the man.

"I'm not sure, but I doubt it. What would he have to gain? I'd say it's more likely someone in competition with us. Regardless, we'll be extra diligent and watch out for each other."

An endeavor he found most intriguing.

six

Two mornings later, Tab hurried to greet the wagon as it pulled up to their claim. She'd been working her regular quadrant all morning and had just taken a water break when she heard the sound of approaching horses. Dust swirled around them and made her cough, but she waved it away, eager for the first glimpse of her father.

His illness had aged him in the brief time he'd been gone. Or maybe she'd been too busy during the past couple of weeks to notice his decline. She hadn't realized how thin he'd become. His sunken eyes sought hers, but he didn't hold their contact. Instead, he busied himself with stepping down from the wagon, refusing the hands offered him.

Hunter appeared beside Tab, and she welcomed his quiet strength.

"C'mon, Papa, let's get you settled over here." She motioned toward the chair Hunter had so thoughtfully brought over the night before. "You can supervise me as I work, and we can talk and catch up."

Her father stood silently before her, contemplative as he surveyed their claim.

"Or if you'd rather, you could lie down for a bit after your trip out here. I'm sure it wasn't pleasant to be bumped around after your illness."

"I'd rather you stop fussing and leave me alone. I'll make the decisions on what I do or don't do next."

Her father's words, clipped and abrupt, cut through her.

"I—I'm sorry." She stepped back, blinking away tears. She didn't want Hunter and the other men around them to see her pain.

Hunter stepped in, saving her further humiliation by addressing the men who had wandered over to check out the new arrival. "There's nothing to see here. You can all go back to work. Dr. Augustine is fine."

The men drifted off, but Tabitha held her spot, staring at her father with confusion. Maybe the bad disposition had to do with his episode. Or maybe he'd taken medications that caused him to act in such a hurtful manner. But she knew if nothing else, the behavior was completely out of character. Maybe if she ignored it, he'd get better and things would return to the way they used to be.

"Well, if you don't need anything else, I'll return to my work." She turned her back to him and left Hunter to pick up any pieces.

Though her hands were busy, her mind wouldn't stop analyzing her father's peculiar behavior. She and her father were close, and this new side of him broke her heart. She'd always been the center of his world, and he hers. But from the moment they'd arrived here, his attitude had changed. She hesitated and rocked back onto her heels, deep in thought. Now that she considered things, he'd actually changed in the month or so before their arrival. His lack of enthusiasm began after reading a note, delivered to their door, weeks before the dig began. She'd asked him about it at the time, but he crumpled it angrily in his hand and threw it into the fireplace.

Tabitha forced her cramped muscles to stretch and stood to her feet. She nervously ran her hands over her skirt to smooth it before approaching her father. Thanks to Hunter, at least he now rested in the hardwood chair.

"Father, will you please tell me what's going on? You've not been yourself for a while now. I remember a note that was delivered to you in town just after our arrival in Utah. Did it have anything to do with the dig?"

Her father closed his eyes a moment before looking at her in exasperation. "Must you ask so many questions all the time? Can't you just leave a man alone with his thoughts?"

"You taught me to ask questions. You've always said questions are the basis of science and our reason for living. We ask questions so that we can seek an answer, which gives us purpose in life. Now you want me to stop?" She folded her arms and glared. "I don't understand you anymore. You haven't been yourself this entire dig. Please help me understand what has changed."

"I've changed. It's that simple. I think we need to pack up and go back East. It's time for me to settle down and find you a husband. You need to have a stable life and settle in one place. I'm taking a teaching job at a university." For the first time, he looked directly into her eyes. "We're pulling out and moving home. Your grandmother's house is available. As soon as we can pack up, we'll head that way."

"You can't be serious!" Tabitha hadn't expected this. "We're here. We're in the middle of something we've dreamed about for years. Please talk to me, Father. Help me to understand what has stolen your dream."

"I am serious, and I don't need to explain things to you. We're pulling out as soon as we can. I've already arranged for our passage on the train. We need to be at the station in three days."

Tabitha, for the first time ever, dug in her heels and took a stance against her father. "I'm not going."

Her father's face registered his shock. "You have to go. They aren't going to let you stay here without a male escort. It isn't safe."

Tabitha contemplated his words. He had a point. Joey had pretty much told her the same thing two days before. "Then I'll find an escort, a chaperone."

She bent her knees to bring herself to his eye level and grabbed his hands, so thin and cold in her own. "Father, just help me understand. We've wanted this for so long. We've been on other explorations, and we've learned so much, but never have we been able to be in on the beginning of something this grand. You wanted that award as badly as I still do. What's happened? What's changed?"

"A lot, but I don't feel I have to go into it with you." He pulled his hands from her grasp and eased to his feet before slowly shuffling to their tent.

A sob caught in her throat. She didn't know how to break through his hard shell. He was a stranger. He even walked like an old man as he entered the canvas flap. A heavy burden pressed hard against his chest, and it broke her heart that she couldn't fix it.

Tab glanced up at the cliffs looming over their site, the place where someone had stood to roll a huge stone over the edge and had sent her father into this deep dark place. She had a sudden urge to escape the mundane work of the dig and to go to the highest place. Maybe she'd try to talk to God. Maybe He'd hear her if she got close enough to Him. She wasn't sure, but she knew she had to try.

❧

Hunter watched as Tabitha walked up the dirt road and

turned at the far end, moving out of his sight as she rounded the last tent. The day promised to be hot like the others, but dark clouds lingered on the horizon. He didn't know if rain would be a refreshing, welcome respite from the heat, or if it would only make their work area a muddy mess, but as he'd inadvertently listened to Tabitha and her father talk, he felt an oppression that weighed heavier than any storm.

When Tabitha's father didn't reappear from the tent to go after her, Hunter set down his work tools with a sigh. The direction in which she'd headed led out of camp, and though he didn't know what she had in mind, he knew that without her being familiar with the terrain and area, she wasn't safe alone. He also knew that if any of the other men, especially the more unscrupulous ones, saw her leave on her own, she wouldn't be safe.

Actions like this proved her father right in that she needed to leave with him and not stick around to make such poor choices. She wouldn't be happy, but he intended to set her straight and back her father's decision for her to leave the site. The thought made him sad. The dig would be infinitely more boring without her cheery talk, feisty comebacks, and spontaneous ways. But her leaving would also be more conducive to returning his focus to the task at hand, something he should be doing at this very moment, when instead he now plodded along behind a runaway daughter whose actions seemed to constantly overrule his better judgment.

He stopped short as he realized he'd lost sight of her. His heart skipped a few beats before a shower of rock from above had him looking heavenward.

"Tabitha, what on earth are you thinking climbing up the bluff like that?" He decided in that instant her father had probably suffered a minor heart dysfunction from the many years of trying to keep up with his wayward daughter. How the older man managed to keep up with her as long as he had, Hunter didn't know.

"Oh—Hunter!" Her foot slipped and sent a few more rocks tumbling down his way.

He stepped backward to avoid them and shaded his eyes with his hand. She'd managed to find a sort of path that led up the bluff and apparently intended to climb it to the top.

"You startled me." She'd regained her footing and now clung to the side of the cliff. "What are you doing out here?"

"I think the question would better be asked, what are *you* doing out here?" He tucked his thumbs in his waistband, determined to talk her down. How on earth did a person go from arguing with her father to climbing a cliff that led to nothing but the heavens?

"I need to get away, to think."

She said it so simplistically, as if her need to think explained everything.

"And you can't do that from down here on the ground?" He glanced around at the vast, open desert that surrounded them. "Are there no other quiet places where you can gather your thoughts without putting your pretty little neck at risk?"

She'd continued to climb and now had reached the top. He decided his inactivity only put him at a disadvantage, so began to follow her ascent with his own.

"You think my neck is pretty? What an odd thing to say." Her voice wound over the top of the cliff, where she now sat, and drifted down to him. "I could understand 'pretty eyes' or 'pretty face,' but 'pretty little neck' doesn't really work."

He considered changing his statement, because right about

now he only wanted to throttle her pretty little neck, but he waited to voice the comment until he reached the top of the treacherous climb. In hindsight, now that he was committed to the endeavor, he couldn't believe she'd kept her grip when he'd startled her moments before. It took every bit of his concentration to keep from slipping and falling. A fall like this would guarantee at the very least a broken leg when landing on the hard-packed ground below. He reached the top, pulled himself up over the edge, and lay on his back while staring up at her.

Guileless blue eyes returned his stare.

He shook his head. "That was stupid."

She nodded. "But you had to do it, didn't you?"

"I meant on your part."

"Well, that's a matter of opinion. I considered it necessary."

He pushed to his elbows. "What would make a dangerous climb like that 'necessary'? You said you wanted to think. Is there no other place—a place safe and on solid ground that doesn't entail a forty-foot drop—for you to give way to your thoughts?"

She shrugged. "I'm sure there is, but at the moment, I could only think of getting up here. I needed to be able to have complete aloneness." She sent him a sideways glare. "You can see how well that worked out."

Pulling her gaze from his, she glanced down and fiddled with her skirt. "I thought if I could get up here, maybe I'd feel closer to God and He'd hear my prayers."

Hunter dropped back to stare at the sky in frustration. "God hears your prayers wherever you are. You don't have to risk life or limb to get to Him. He's everywhere you are. A quiet prayer uttered from the safety of my chair would have been just as effective as one uttered on this bluff."

"Really?" The corner of her mouth tipped up into an alluring grin. "Now you tell me."

"Yes, really." He pushed to a sitting position and scouted out the area. At least no rattlers sunned on the platform with them. But his thoughts went in dangerous directions with Tabitha sitting so close and with them being so alone. He wondered what it would be like to kiss her, while they were alone up here without all the prying eyes that had followed their every move at camp—a temptation that showed him exactly why they needed to stay under the watchful eyes at camp.

He stood and hurried away from her and the alluring thoughts. "Look, footprints."

Though the sandstone was hard, a soft powdery dust covered the outcropping, and a path of footprints led to the edge on the eastern side.

Tabitha reached for his hand and, in a moment of triumph, he walked back to help her to her feet. A week or so earlier she would have tried to bite any hand offered to her. She rolled her eyes at his smug grin but kept his hand gripped tightly in her own.

They followed the footprints to the edge and looked down. The entire dig spread out before them, the workers looking small from this vantage point. Everyone was intent on the ground below them. Not one person looked up to see them standing there, which had worked in Tab's attacker's favor when he'd pushed the rock over and onto the tent. Hunter tightened his hold on her hand as the picture passed through his mind of what could have been.

"Your father's right, you know. You need to leave the area

with him. You aren't safe here."

She caught her breath with a fast intake of air. "You don't want me here? I thought you'd offer to watch out for me, that you'd want to keep me here as badly as I want to stay."

She pulled her hand away, and he suddenly felt bereft and alone.

"I want you safe. Someone stood on this very cliff and had taken the time and forethought into getting that huge rock up here. It wasn't a spur of the moment deal, nor done on a whim. Someone wanted to hurt—or possibly even kill—you."

He crossed his arms over his chest and stared at her. "I don't want you to leave. I've grown fond of you, and I enjoy your presence, but I don't want you to stay with your life at risk."

"I want to win the plaque for my father."

Stubborn woman.

Hunter wasn't in the race for fame or fortune, though he did love the thrill of finding new bones and the challenge of touching history. He liked that his work would further the science of archaeology for others who came after them. Though he didn't understand her determination to do this for recognition only, and to win the event at all costs, he did appreciate her devotion to her father.

"Why?"

She walked away from the edge, away from the eyes that might pry at them from below if someone looked up from their digging for a momentary break. "Because I've watched him work hard his whole life, and he's never once been recognized for that. He lost some prime years to stay with me as a child. Most men would have left their child with the grandmother who wholeheartedly embraced the opportunity.

But he chose to stay. He didn't want me to lose him after losing my mother."

"Then maybe this is the time for you to show him that same concern and do as he asks and leave. I'm sure he'd rather have you over some silly plaque."

She turned to face him, pushing back the blond tendrils that blew free from her braid and drifted across her face. "No. He's not leaving because he wants to. I'm sure of it. If he were, I'd go along with him. But I have a feeling he's leaving because he's being forced to go, and I won't let someone do that to him. I'll stay and fight for the find. . .for the award."

"That doesn't make sense!" Hunter again wanted to throttle her. Here she'd admitted that someone wanted them gone, someone desperate enough that he would go to the extremes of murder to get his way, yet Tab stubbornly wanted to stay and face more potential threats. "You're in danger, and you need to go."

He saw the expression of doubt pass across her features, followed by a look of fear before he realized how harsh his words sounded. She took a nervous step away from him.

"It could be you. You might be the one chasing us out. And here I've foolishly led you right out of camp and onto a desolate and dangerous place."

Hunter couldn't believe she'd think such a thing of him. "It's not me. I followed you so I could protect you."

"But how do I know that for sure? You're just as determined as everyone else to make the find."

"Right. That's why I'm up here arguing with your stubborn little self while the others continue to work below us."

She glanced at the cliff and moved farther away. "If you were to push me, my father would be devastated."

"If I wanted to push you, I'd have done it when we were standing together over there minutes ago. No one would have seen me. You're safe with me, Tabitha. Admit it." He saw the hesitation in her eyes, but she must have realized he had a point. He'd had his moment and didn't take it.

"I'm sorry. I don't know what to think or who to trust anymore. I can't even trust my father's judgment."

"You can trust me, but I still say you need to listen to your father and leave."

"He's always taught me to chase after my dreams. This is one of them. It's his dream, but it's also my dream for us. I'm not leaving."

"Are you sure? I know your father isn't making sense to you—and I can't understand his stance on this either. But he's a great scientist, and I appreciate and respect his work. I don't agree with his thoughts on all his scholarly attitudes, especially when it comes to God, but I do know he's running scared from something, and I'm not sure you want to stick around and find out what it is."

"I'm not leaving."

She'd dug her heels in again, figuratively speaking, and he knew he couldn't pry her from her determination to stay. He reached out his hand, and after a small hesitation, she took it. "You came up here to pray. Let's do that now, together." He pulled her close and held her soft form in his arms while he said the heartfelt words to his Lord. He prayed for her decision, for her father's pain and struggle, and for their protection.

"Hunter, how do you suppose the person responsible for the boulder got it up here?"

"I've wondered that myself. I guess there's a possibility it already waited here. Maybe it fell from one of the higher bluffs."

She voiced her agreement. "There's no way someone carried or dragged it up. Unless they hoisted it?"

"Maybe, but I doubt it."

As he led her back to the ledge to begin their descent, she balked.

"C'mon. I'm not going to hurt you."

"I know. It's not that."

She glanced up at him with a new fear in her eyes and nervously licked her lip. "It's the drop. The distance looked much better from the ground, and I'm not sure now how I'll ever make it back down."

She had a point. The ledge looked nonexistent from up here, and taking the first step into thin air held little attraction for him, either.

"I tell you what. Why don't we scout around a bit and see if we can find another way. If we don't find a safer path, I'll support you and get you safely down."

They walked around the entire perimeter but found no other way off the sandstone bluff.

Hunter sat down at the edge of the cliff where they'd climbed up. "I'll go first, and I'll assist you as you come behind me. It's wider than it looks. It's all an illusion. You're going to have to trust me."

"The ledge might be an illusion, but the forty-foot drop beyond it isn't." She shuddered.

"I'll keep you safe. Just do as I say and trust me." And he'd trust God to watch over them and keep them safe in the same way. He sent up a frantic prayer that Tabitha wouldn't panic and cause a fall that would surely lead to both of their deaths.

He lowered himself over the top ridge and settled onto the firm support of the ledge. He turned and assisted Tabitha in doing the same.

Once they'd made the initial turn, they were fine. He jumped the last few feet to the ground and reached up to lift her down.

"We did it!" Her euphoria was contagious.

"We did."

"I'm sorry I suggested it might be you trying to hurt us and chase us off. I know better."

He waved away her words. "You really don't. But I'll do my best to convince you."

They walked in silence for a few minutes.

"If I'd wanted to hurt you, I could have done something the other day, too. I had the entire morning."

"I thought of that, but everyone knew the two of us were together. It would have been too dangerous. You'd have been the first suspect and would have been caught." Her smile showed him she wasn't serious, at least not anymore. If the thought had crossed her mind, and at some point it apparently had, she'd found peace with it for now.

"Hmm, good point."

They'd reached the site, and no one had missed them this time.

Tabitha touched his arm. "I'm serious about staying, too. I need you to help me. I can't do it without your support."

"We'll worry about it if your father indeed decides to leave. Maybe after he thinks things through, and after seeing your reaction to leaving, he'll change his mind."

"Maybe. But I highly doubt it." She rubbed her hands up and down her arms as goose bumps formed on her flesh.

Though the air felt warm, Hunter also felt the chill. Something was wrong, and he determined to find out what it was. He'd protect Tabitha, no matter what the cost. He'd found a treasure worth more than the dig, something he hadn't expected when he'd originally signed up.

seven

Tabitha woke early the next morning and watched her father sleep. His loud mutterings had wakened her, and she realized the term *sleep* was a stretch as there was nothing restful about the process in his case. He tossed and turned and cried out about treasure and danger. Even in his dreams he battled something unknown. Tabitha listened intently, hoping something he said would give her a clue about the cause of his recent behavior. But she could only decipher a mix of phrases that meant nothing.

When he finally returned to a more restful state, she gave up her own attempt at sleep and climbed out of bed. She stepped behind the hanging sheet they'd rigged for privacy and pulled on a fresh white blouse and tan skirt. Though the colors were practical, she'd already tired of them. She longed to wear some of her prettier clothes, but she'd left most of them behind, knowing the work out here would permanently soil them. The clothes she brought were chosen with care—light, airy fabrics that wouldn't hold the heat any more than necessary and bland colors that were easy to clean.

She laughed inwardly at that thought. Her entire wardrobe carried stains from the work site, and nothing she could imagine would prevent the arid heat from seeping through to her skin. Not for the first time, she wished for a pair of trousers like the men wore. But her father drew the line at that notion. His daughter might work on the sites in a man's world, but she'd do it while wearing the clothes of a lady.

She tried to slip quietly through the tent flap, but her father's snore turned into a waking cough and slowed her. He leaned up on his elbow.

"Tabitha? Where are you going?"

"I'm sorry I woke you, Father. I thought I'd slip out for an early breakfast and get a head start on the day."

He stared past her to gauge the slant of the rising sun. "So you can get a start on the packing, I hope?"

She sighed. "I've not changed my mind. I don't want to leave. I don't plan to leave. I want you to stay, too."

He already shook his head in denial. "No."

"Then please explain to me why. I don't understand what's changed since we arrived. If you'd share your thoughts, your concerns, maybe I'd be able to understand, but. . ." Her voice tapered off, and she held her hands helplessly out at her side as she sank down on her own cot and faced him. "Without knowing what's going on, I can't."

"There are things you don't know and don't need to know. I don't have to explain myself to you."

"But you always have before. And I'm not a child, Papa. I'm an adult. I deserve to know what's behind your departure so I can make an informed decision of my own."

"No." Her father turned away, and she knew that in his opinion the conversation had ended.

"Then I'll remain here, even if you leave."

He returned his stare to her for several long moments and then shrugged. "I won't drag you out of here against your will, but you're making a big mistake."

Tears filled her eyes at the coldness in his tone. His eyes were icy, and she felt no warmth emanating from him at all.

The man before her was still a stranger. She felt more at ease and had more peace when in Hunter's company than at this moment, and since Hunter had rubbed her wrong from the moment she met him, that said a lot.

She refused to cry. "Where will you go?"

"I'll head in to town. If you need me, inquire at the general store. I'll let them know where I'll be. I have some research I can attend to until you come to your senses, which I dare to suggest won't be long. In the meantime, I'll delay our train tickets."

"Father, I fully intend to stay here until the dig is over. That could be days, or it could be weeks."

"Well, whenever that is, you know where to find me. I'll have to borrow a horse since the supply wagon isn't heading to town for several days. I'll leave most of my things and the supplies here with you."

Tabitha nodded and hurried through the tent flap to the welcoming breeze outside. The early morning sky already caused her to squint with its brilliant blue colors. And without a cloud to block it, the sun shone directly into her eyes. She lifted her hat and placed it on her head.

Talk to Me and pray. The unbidden words carried so clearly to her that Tabitha looked around to see if Hunter stood nearby. But she stood alone. No one else moved about this early. She considered the gentle command. *Talk to Me and pray.*

The words brought with them the urge to talk to God. The long day loomed ahead of her and would continue to pass, while her dilemma simmered deep inside. She thought of her prayer the day before with Hunter and for a moment considered returning to her cliff, but the memory that the trip down wasn't an easy one even with Hunter at her side caused her to stay put. She knew her best plan would be to place one foot in front of the other and continue making progress, both figuratively and emotionally, on what she needed to do. So instead of heading toward the cliff, she headed toward the empty tables of the dining area. The cook would begin his preparations soon, and she'd eat and get right to work. But in the meantime, she'd listen to the tiny voice and pray.

⋅ð⋅

"Huh-uh. No way." Hunter held up his hand and interrupted her plea for assistance before she could get anymore inane words past her pretty little lips. "We've already been through this. If your father says you need to leave, you need to leave. It's settled."

Tabitha sent him her most stubborn glare, and he knew he was in trouble. "It's not settled, at least not between you and me. As to my father and I, yes, you're right. He's leaving, and I'm staying. That's the only thing that's been agreed upon."

"The committee will send you packing in his tracks. You heard what Joey said the other day. The only reason he changed his mind and backed off is because we pushed, knowing your father's return was imminent. Now that he's leaving again, the situation has changed."

"Not for me it hasn't. I signed on for the dig, and they accepted me."

"As a partner to your father."

"Nowhere in my paperwork does it state that."

"But it's implied."

"Implied where?" She crossed her arms over her chest and stared him down. "I've seen no rules stating such a thing. There's no mention of women not working alone anywhere in the paperwork. And trust me, I've been through it all."

He imagined she had been. The woman was nothing if not meticulous. "But the committee will state the information on women isn't there because they've never had an issue with it. No woman has dared to step foot in their world or question their process."

"Until now."

He sighed. "Until now."

"I've already told my father, and now I'm telling you. I'm staying. I can do this with your support and backing, or I can stay without it."

Her words caused visual after visual to pass through his mind. If she stayed without her father's protection—or his—she'd be at the mercy of any of the scoundrels who filled the camp. Her reputation would be sullied, not that she seemed to care at this point. And whoever had already made attempts on her life would have free rein to try another attack. And worse, but most important to him, he didn't know if he'd ever see her again if she left, nor would he have the chance to speak further to her about the Lord.

"I'm not going to sway you on this, am I?" His weary tone gave away the fact that he hovered on the verge of giving in. The way her face lit up at the question proved she didn't miss that little fact.

"Nope." She stepped closer, hope filling her eyes for the first time. "Look. I have the book knowledge, and you have the field knowledge."

"I have book knowledge, too. I studied at the university back in St. Louis."

"Oh, I'm so sorry. I didn't mean to insult you." She tipped a grin his way. "And I've never actually studied at the university level. After my short stay at the preparatory school, my father felt it best I continue my studies with him. Regardless, if we work together, I know we'll make a good team."

Resignation battled with concern. "Then I'll head over to speak with your father, and you'd best get to work. I'll let you know what he says. If he's agreeable, we'll work the claims as a team."

She grabbed his arms in a quick hug before she caught herself and looked around. "Sorry. But thank you. You won't regret this."

Hunter was sure that in some way or another, he surely would.

❧

Two days later, Hunter found himself questioning why he'd ever made such a harebrained decision to help Tab. When she wasn't hard at work, she talked. Incessantly. When he needed to talk, she held up her hand for silence while working on inanely delicate procedures that made him want to pull his hair out. At the rate she worked, they wouldn't find anything of relevance for at least another decade.

"I don't know why you're all bent out of shape over my methods. It's not like you had someone faster to work with before I came along. You should look at everything I do as a bonus." Tabitha stood and peered at him, hands on hips, looking truly confused about his frustration.

"But the deal was you'd be an asset to my 'team,' and as it is, your work method looks like you're picking fleas out of an old hound dog. We aren't going to make progress or win any competition at this rate. If you work any slower, people will think you're taking a nap." Hunter grabbed his sledgehammer and stomped over to the farthest edge of his work area. He didn't miss the fact that she rolled her eyes and went back to her own area with a frustrated huff. She kicked an innocent rock high into the air before she settled back into place.

Hunter swung the sledgehammer up and back over his head with more force than he'd meant to use. He was thrown off balance by the sudden lightness as the head flew off the wooden end and catapulted through the air, barely missing Tabitha's bent form. She screeched and jumped to her feet after it whizzed past. They both watched in shock as it tore through her tent and landed inside with a thud. Her face paled of all color.

"What on earth are you trying to do?" Her shriek pierced through his ears. His head began to pound. "You could have killed me."

"The confounded thing flew off. It's not like I did it on purpose." He strode over to her tent and pulled back the flap to see that the iron had embedded itself in the dirt floor. He stepped inside, pulled it out of the ground, and picked it up, bringing it outside for his perusal.

Tabitha peered over his shoulder. "Did it wear out from use? How old is that thing anyway?"

"I bought it new for this expedition, and for the price I paid, it should have lasted for years." He turned the heavy item over in his hand and compared it to the piece of wood he still clutched in his other hand. "If that don't beat all. Look here."

He pointed to the place where the head had attached to the wood handle.

Tabitha did as he said. "Okay. What am I looking for?"

"See this streak on the wood? It's a scrape. Someone pried the head loose. This wasn't an accident." He raised his eyes and met her concerned gaze.

She contemplated his words a moment before disbelief filled her eyes. "What are you saying? Someone purposely pried it loose, just hoping this would happen? Or worse, that you'd hit me with it? What are the chances. . . ?"

"I'm serious, Tab. Someone did this on purpose."

Another cloud of concern passed over her face. "How do I know it wasn't you?"

"Right. I tampered with my own tools. I damaged one of my most important pieces of gear on purpose. I'm doing that to self-sabotage, and if I can aim at you in the process, that gives me bonus points." It was his turn to face her with hands on hips. He couldn't begin to figure how to show her the level of frustration she brought out in him. "C'mon, Tabitha, give me one good reason as to why I'd tamper with my own tools. That doesn't even begin to make sense."

She flinched. "Sorry."

He stared her down. "I could just as easily accuse you, you know. I didn't have any problems until you joined me. And you're the one so determined to get the plaque with your name on it."

"*Me?*"

Her indignant gasp shot through the air, and even with the severity of what had just happened, he battled an urge to smile.

She glared, and the color returned to her cheeks. "I think not. What would I have to gain?"

"Exactly my point to you. We're a team."

"Then let's get back to it." She stalked over to his site but tossed her final words at him from across her shoulder. "And for the record, it's my *father's* name I want to see on the plaque, not mine."

eight

"Tabitha, have you seen my chisel? I had it right over here before we went for lunch." Hunter turned in a circle, a perplexed expression on his face. Three weeks into the dig, this Monday afternoon had been nothing but one slow down after another.

After wiping her hands on her skirt, an act she regretted when she noticed the streaks of mud her sweaty hands left there, Tabitha sat back and glanced at her partner. "No, I have my own chisel. Why would I need yours?"

"I don't know." Hands on hips, he continued to glance around his work area. "I thought maybe you needed it for some reason. Hmm, this is odd. I know I left it right here when we went to eat." He turned in another circle, surveying their work areas.

Tabitha shrugged and went back to her own work. She'd found a few fossils that looked promising and didn't want to be distracted.

She could hear him tossing a few tools around and digging through his bins and boxes of equipment. The noise distracted her, and she wished he'd settle in.

When it became apparent that wasn't going to happen until he found his beloved chisel, she called out to him. "You're welcome to use mine."

"Or...I could use mine," he stated from right behind her.

She about jumped out of her skin. "Oh good, you found it."

When he didn't answer, she turned around to look up at him. He had a funny expression on his face.

"What?" She stood. "Is something wrong? Where'd you find it?"

"Where indeed?" He continued to appraise her, something akin to doubt in his eyes.

"Hunter, I don't have time to play guessing games. What's the problem?"

He flipped the chisel over and over in his hands. "I found it in your box."

"In *my* box? Well, I surely didn't put it there. I went to lunch with you, remember? When would I have had a chance to sneak back here and tamper with your chisel?"

"You left for a few moments. . ." His voice drifted off, his meaning clear.

She reached back and ran her fingers over her hair. "I only took a trip to the. . .well, you know. . .a trip to take care of necessities. You think I faked that so I could make a side trip over here to hide your chisel where you'd find it in my box? And how would I have sneaked past the table with you sitting there? The kitchen area backs up to the cliff. Or wait, you saw my agility on the cliff the other day—maybe I climbed up that way? Did I drop off the bluff over there?"

"It does sound a bit silly when you put it that way. But I can do without the sarcasm."

"But honestly, Hunter. How do you think it feels to be accused of such a silly thing? You should know me better by now."

"I do. And I'm sorry. But you have to admit, things keep happening since we've joined forces, and that's kind of odd when nothing of the sort happened before."

"Nothing of the sort? What do you call someone pushing a rock over onto my tent? That's not exactly an everyday occurrence." Though he had a point. Since they'd become partners, strange things kept happening at regular intervals. Items went missing. Then the missing items turned up in the oddest places. The sledgehammer had been tampered with, and other items disappeared completely. Hunter once walked into his tent, and the entire thing collapsed on top of him. Though she had to admit, the bewildered expression on his face when he'd poked his head back out through the opening after flailing around inside for a few moments had sent her into gales of laughter. That didn't mean she had anything to do with it.

"So you admit, the trouble seems to come where you're concerned, not me."

"Ohh." He was back to that again. She stalked over to her side of the work site before swinging around to face him. "I'll admit no such thing. I can just as easily blame you. If you scare both my father and me off, you'll have this whole area to yourself. Maybe that's what's going on here. You know we've chosen a prime area for the find."

"If that was my intent, why did I agree to watch over you, which is the only reason your father allowed you to stay?"

She hesitated for a moment and thought that question over. "So you'd look innocent while casting blame on me, as a woman, for the odd things that keep happening."

They were at a standoff. She didn't know how she could possibly work with him a moment longer. *The man is insufferable.*

"I kept you here because I enjoy your company."

Aw. . .and he can be sweet, too. She amended her previous thought.

"And I kept you here because of the importance you said the event held for your father. Though I have to say, if that's the case, he sure has a funny way of showing it."

She couldn't dispute that. He had a valid point.

He eyed her, his face pensive. "I've wondered about something since your father left."

"What?" She walked over to settle in Hunter's chair.

"Why'd he leave you behind? If he felt so strongly about leaving, why did he give in to me so easily when I asked about you staying?"

Tabitha sent him a wry grin. "I tend to be a tad stubborn. He knew he'd face a losing battle."

Hunter let loose with a belly laugh. "That has to be the understatement of the year."

Tabitha determined that she liked the sound of Hunter's laughter. She decided she'd work extra hard to make sure she heard it often.

⁂

Though it hadn't rained since Hunter's arrival at the dig, heavy clouds promised this day would be different. The oppressive humidity hung over the camp, making tempers flare. Several fights had broken out, and they could hear raised voices from across the way that signaled the start of another fiasco.

Tabitha had kept to herself, quietly focusing on the closest corner of her father's dig. She'd taken to moving from one spot to another, her randomness a complete change from the focused methodical path she'd taken when working with her father. Apparently, she found the freedom refreshing.

"Tell me something." After watching her for a while, Hunter couldn't keep silent a moment longer.

She whipped her head around, a startled expression showing

how intent she'd been before he'd interrupted. "What?"

"You've changed your whole work process. Could you fill me in on your thoughts?"

"Oh. Well." She stood and shook the dust from her skirt and arms. "We've been at this for weeks and haven't gotten anywhere. I figure if I keep at it with that method, I'll never find the right area."

She glanced around at the many holes that covered the dirt in front of her and grinned over at him. "I guess I have skipped around a bit. But I'm finding some promising signs over there, so I won't move on until I've fully investigated it." She pointed at the location.

"Really? Show me."

Hunter followed her to the spot and hunkered down beside her. He was close enough that he could smell the scent of flowers emanating from her hair, a most surprising revelation. He'd found her to be all business, so this feminine attribute caught him completely off guard for a moment.

"Did you hear me?" She nudged him with her boot. "You didn't hear a word I just said. Where'd your mind disappear to?"

"Sorry. I got distracted." He felt a flush move up his neck.

"Anyway, as I said, if you look closely, the first sign of life is embedded in the ground right there."

He peered to where she pointed, and his heart leaped with excitement. "You're right! This is wonderful. Why didn't you call me over immediately?"

She looked at him warily. "I wanted to be sure. It's not like I was holding out on you or anything."

"I didn't mean. . ."

A shout from across the way interrupted their conversation. "I've found it! I discovered the first bone! I've won!"

The dismay on Tabitha's face reflected the disappointment that flooded Hunter at the man's words. He helped her to her feet, and they walked over reluctantly to see what the man had uncovered.

Hunter had to admit his first thought was that Tabitha now would return to her father and they'd head off to parts unknown, far away from him. The disappointment of that realization far overshadowed the fact that he'd not been the one to win. But as they moved closer, a certain excitement seeped through him. History had been made again, and they were close to seeing the remains of the huge creatures that had once walked the same area where they now stood.

Joey pushed through the crowd as they circled the winner's encampment. "Everyone move back. Out of the way, please. I need to get through here. Let me see what you have."

The crowd parted, and Joey took the item the man held exuberantly in his hands. He surveyed it for long moments. Everyone waited in anticipation. A crack of thunder had everyone jumping, so intense was their concentration on hearing what Joey would have to say.

"What is it? Can you tell?" Tabitha asked from beside Hunter. Though she stood on her toes, she couldn't begin to see over the towering heads of the men in front of them.

"No, I can't see anything. It's a small bone, but they're holding it down low, and I can't get a glimpse of it from here."

More long moments passed, and the crowd grew impatient.

"Let someone look at it who actually knows about these things," one man called out from the back.

Cheers of agreement echoed around them.

Hunter could hear frustration in Joey's muffled reply.

Thunder rolled again, this time much closer. The storm seemed to be moving fast. Black clouds filled the sky and moved rapidly their way. Tabitha moved a step closer to Hunter.

"I don't think this is going to be like the storm we saw from atop the bluff."

"I don't either." Hunter tried to mask his worry. Storms out here were vicious, and all they had for protection were flimsy tents. It wouldn't be proper for either one of them to be unchaperoned in the other's tent, so they'd have to take cover alone. With Tabitha's move toward him at the thunder's loud boom, he didn't think she'd feel safe after she left his side. He said a quick prayer for their safety and for her peace. Maybe the storm would divert.

As the storm neared, the crowd echoed the tension.

"I've got to get closer. Maybe if I see the bones, I can help identify them." Tabitha began to work her way through the throng of men, and Hunter stayed close at her heels. He wasn't taking any chances in this mob of losing her. If the bone had indeed been found, the event would be over and a lot of disappointed men would have reason to act out.

As they neared the front, they could see Joey looking at the object in his hand with consternation.

Without seeming to give thought to what she was doing, Tabitha walked right up to him. "Mr. Matthews, if you don't mind, I might be able to help identify this if you'll let me look at it."

Joey all but thrust the object into her hands. Hunter watched her face with interest as she perused the bone from all sides. She pulled it close where she peered intently at it for several more moments before sending a strange look Joey's way.

"May I speak with you in private?"

Joey nodded. He took her by the arm and led her away from the crowd.

Hunter followed.

"Mr. Pierce, the lady specifically asked to speak with me alone, if you don't mind."

"It just so happens, I do mind. I have a commitment to her father to watch over her at all times."

Tabitha waved their words away. "I don't mind Hunter staying. This isn't about him."

Joey returned his focus to her. "Then what is it about? Why didn't you just tell me the name of the bone over there? I'm sure the entire crowd is anxious to hear what we have."

"Well, that's just the problem. This bone isn't from here."

"What are you saying?" Joey's face reflected his confusion.

"I'm saying exactly what I mean. The bone isn't from here. It's a counterfeit."

Joey had the audacity to laugh. Hunter had the audacity to want to punch him in the face.

"You're surely mistaken. Why would the man have reason to pull out a fake bone?"

"Why, indeed? You'll have to ask him that question. I'd venture a guess that he wants to win, and by bringing his own bone along, he'd have a sure thing."

"Unless we have a resident expert on hand, which we do." Hunter's pride carried through his words.

"He'd have to know we'd have an expert look it over anyway," Joey spat. "I'm sure you mean well, Miss Augustine, but I'll have to take this to the committee before we can resume the dig or accuse one of our fine scientists of such a severe crime."

Tabitha shrugged. "Suit yourself." She handed the bone over without another glance. "But if you'll look at the plaster caked on the end, you'll see that I'm correct without making a fool of yourself in front of 'your committee.'"

Joey's face burned red as he saw the blob of plaster she'd pointed out to him.

"Also, the density isn't at all appropriate for such a small bone. The entire thing is wrong."

This time the crack of thunder and following strike of lightning raised the hairs on Hunter's neck. The following roar and blast of wind that followed signaled that a downpour was imminent.

"Everyone to their tents, and hurry! We aren't safe standing out here in the open." Joey hurried toward the crowd without a backward glance.

The rain swept over them, and everyone's eyes were on the bone as it began to fall apart. Tabitha's mouth quirked up at the corners as Hunter took her arm and tried to move her in the direction of their tents. "You might want to hurry up yourself and get that in a dry spot before it melts completely and you have nothing left to show the committee."

Joey's expression of fury matched that of the oncoming storm.

☙

Tabitha ducked into her tent and felt relief to see that the entire interior had stayed dry. She closed the flap against the wind and slipped her wet clothing up over her head. After pulling on a dry nightdress, she hung the wet objects around the tent so they wouldn't mildew. Though it was early evening, the tent had darkened considerably with the weather, and Tabitha found the need to light her oil lamp.

She found a book to study and turned to settle on her cot. A strange white envelope lay on her pillow, and her heart skipped a beat with excitement. Only Hunter would have entered her tent and thought to do something so bold. She'd been careful to hide her growing feelings for him, not sure how he'd react, but maybe he'd decided to make the first move and declare his feelings for her.

Her hands shook as she tore open the envelope, her fingers awkward with excitement. Finally, the single page slipped out, and she opened it with trembling fingers. She settled down onto the cot and leaned nearer the lantern in order to see the tiny print that covered only the top portion of the letter. Tamping down her disappointment that it was so short, she reminded herself there'd be plenty of time for Hunter to work into longer missives. She began to read the words, and her heart sank with dread.

The letter wasn't in any way Hunter's declaration of his love. Instead, she read a threat that said in no uncertain terms that Tabitha was to pull out and leave the competition or her father would face dire circumstances. She had no doubt as to the meaning of the statement. A shiver passed through her at the pure evil in the intent of the note.

She had no idea how long she sat there, but a tap on her tent made her jump, and she realized the rain had finally tapered off to a drizzle.

"Tabitha? I just wanted to check on you. Are you doing okay? The storm seems to have passed, and I've brought you a plate of dinner."

"Just a moment. I'll be right out." She heard the tremor in her own voice and knew Hunter would think it left over from the storm. She hurried to dress in a dry outfit before joining him outside. The dusky sky left just enough light for them to see each other well. The refreshing scent of new rain filled the air. She wondered how the air could smell so sweet when someone among them breathed evil into it.

One look at her face and she could tell Hunter sensed something more than a storm had upset her.

"What is it, Tab?"

She held out the paper she clutched tightly in her hand. She watched Hunter's reaction as he read. As the realization of the threat passed over his features, she knew without a doubt he'd had nothing to do with its arrival. Besides the obvious fact that they'd been together the whole time leading up to her finding it, his emotions made it clear.

"That's it, honey. You have to get out of here. I can't let you stay when we know someone has a personal vendetta against you. I can't keep you safe when I don't know who the person is who would do something like this."

"If I run, if he chases me off, he wins. I can't let him win, Hunter. My father received a note. . . . What if it was similar to this one and that's why he's been acting so strange? Are we all going to quit the dig one by one until the coward who would do this claims the prize? I won't stand for it."

Hunter stared at her a moment. "I can see where the stubborn part comes in. I don't stand a chance on convincing you to leave, do I?"

"Absolutely not. I won't be chased away."

"Then we need to take this to Joey. He's not going to be happy, especially after you pointed out the fallacy of his melting bone."

She actually giggled, which in turn mortified her. She hadn't giggled since girlhood. "At least I pointed it out in private."

Hunter tried to hide his own grin. "Yes, but I'm not sure he'll see it that way. Being bettered by anyone doesn't seem to set well with the man. But regardless, he needs to know about this."

She took the plate he'd brought her and set it inside where she'd eat it after they returned.

"Thank you for not giving up on me," she told Hunter as they walked.

"It's against my better judgment, but we'll be extra diligent. I want to be with you wherever you go. Promise me you'll not step foot out of this camp again unless I'm at your side."

"I promise." It wasn't exactly the declaration of love she'd wanted earlier, but she'd be content with his desire to protect her. With him by her side, watching her so carefully, what else could possibly go wrong?

nine

Tabitha opened her eyes and tried to see through the pressing darkness. Though the air hung silent and heavy and not a sound reached her ears, the hair on the back of her neck stood up. Something—or someone—had wakened her, and she felt sure the vague movement or brushing noise had come from the interior of her pitch-black tent.

"Hunter?"

She whispered his name into the darkness, even though she knew he'd never enter her tent without a chaperone, let alone have reason to sneak around in the dark.

A chill ran up her arms, and she hugged them tightly against her chest. If only she could see; even a dim outline of her surroundings would be helpful. Most nights, depending on the moon, she could see pretty well, but tonight, due to the clouds that still remained after the storm, she couldn't see a thing.

Hesitantly, she sat up on her cot. She cringed as the wood and canvas-shrouded apparatus squeaked in protest, the sound loud in the oppressive quiet. When she froze in place, a soft shuffling noise reached her ears, barely discernible, but there nonetheless. Her airway seemed to close off, and she felt as though she couldn't breathe.

"Who's there?" her fear-filled words rasped out from the tightness of her dry throat. "Please, tell me what you want."

Nothing. Only silence and the beating of her heart reached

her ears. There wasn't any answer. Only her labored, terror-filled breathing cut through the silence. She wondered if she could have been on the verge of a nightmare when she'd awakened. Maybe the noise had filled her dreams, not her reality.

She sat motionless for a few more moments and with a sigh of relief realized that must have been exactly what had happened. Already on edge from her father's desertion, and then the storm and threat, it only made sense that she would be nervous. The unease carried over into her dreams and had in this case turned into a nightmare. She swung her legs over the side of the cot and onto the cool dirt floor.

She'd noticed that though the days were hot and arid, the nights were pleasant and at times even chilly. A breath of fresh air would do wonders to slow her beating heart and put to rest some of the fears running rampant through her. She'd not realized how vulnerable she'd feel without her father's protective presence beside her.

She felt around for the robe she'd placed on the trunk at the end of her bed and slipped it on as she stood. Though she couldn't see, she knew the way to the entry of her tent. With only her cot and her father's, both in opposite corners across from each other, and then a trunk for each of them for clothes and personal items pushed against the ends of the beds, there wasn't a lot of furniture to weave around or worry about. She'd moved a crate of books over to his side, and now she had even more clear space to walk through.

As she reached for the canvas flap, a rough hand grasped her upper arm while the other yanked her backward and wrapped around her mouth. She screamed, but the gloved hand masked the noise. Her entire body trembled in terror.

A gravelly whisper reached her as the man murmured into her ear. "So, does *Mr.* Pierce make it a habit to sneak into your tent in the dark of night? No wonder you two seem so chummy."

Tabitha took advantage of the moment and slammed her elbow back into the man's ribs. Though he grunted in pain, he rewarded her action by tightening his grip on her upper arm. She cried out in pain. His hand pressed tighter against her mouth, too, and with the edge of his glove pressing against her nose, she could hardly breathe. She panicked. Her father couldn't lose her this way. He'd never forgive himself. Whatever the man wanted, she had to survive this attack.

"I'm going to remove my hand from your mouth, but if you so much as cry out, I'll hurt you. Do you understand?"

After her nod, he moved his hand slightly away, and she gasped in the welcome breaths of air.

She caught her breath and then hissed, "Hunter has never so much as stepped foot in my tent, other than to retrieve the top of his sledgehammer in the light of day. How dare you accuse him—or me—of anything less than stellar behavior?" She had no clue why she felt the need to clear the air at such a time, but the man's insinuation bothered her.

Again the man's grip tightened around her arm. He now held her tightly against his chest, his free arm having slipped down from her mouth to curve around her neck. Did he plan to strangle her? What could he possibly have as a reason to hurt her?

"Oh really, then why would you cry out for him in the dark?" The man's snide chuckle wrapped around her. "It sounded to me as if you expected his little midnight visit."

"You're despicable. I heard a noise, and he'd be the least of my worries. Unfortunately, it wasn't him, was it? Now I demand you tell me what you want. I want you out of my tent immediately."

He didn't answer, and a feeling of dread coursed through Tabitha. Anger boiled and made her brave. If he'd come to hurt her, surely he'd have acted immediately. Since he hadn't, his intent must be to scare her.

"I want you out of here, now. Leave my tent at once."

Again, her words only met with silence. She wanted to scream, as much in frustration as terror, though terror had the upper hand.

He leaned close, and she held her breath. "You're not safe here, and you need to leave. You've been warned." She tried not to gag as his fetid breath filled her nose.

After grabbing her by the arms, he spun her around and flung her toward the far side of the tent while he made his quick exit through the doorway.

Not wanting to take any more chances, Tabitha took advantage of the moment and called for Hunter. The sound pierced the darkness that surrounded her.

❧

Hunter flew off his cot at the sound of Tabitha's terror. He pulled on his clothes at a run and reached her tent as neighboring men poured out of theirs. Tripping over the corner rope, he stumbled and caught himself before hurrying around to the front.

"Tabitha, I'm here."

His heart skipped a few beats when she didn't answer, but after a few moments, she pulled the flap open and hurried into his arms.

"It's all right, you're safe. What happened? Did you have a nightmare?"

She pulled away from his embrace, wrapped her arms around her midsection, and seemed to be in shock. At his question, she snapped out of whatever stupor she'd been in and shook her head. "No."

A tear trickled down her porcelain cheek, and she was paler than ever in the overcast moonlight. "Someone came into my tent." Her voice caught in a sob.

"Oh, honey." Hunter pulled her close, not caring what the others thought at the moment. They were well chaperoned. "Are you hurt? Did he. . . ?"

Already she shook her head in answer. "He only grabbed me and whispered in my ear. He said. . .he said. . .I've been warned and I need to leave." Another sob stopped her words. She reached up and mindlessly rubbed her upper arm.

Someone brought a lantern over and set it on the chair beside them. Hunter set her away from him and pushed up her sleeve. Several red welts covered her upper arms. Anger coursed through him. Only the most cowardly of cowards would sneak into a lone woman's sleeping quarters and threaten her in the dark of night.

He leaned close. "Did he hurt you anywhere else?"

"No." Her voice came out as a whisper, a far cry from the strong voice of the woman he'd met on the first day at the dig.

How dare the man take away her confidence and security?

"Will you be okay for a few minutes? I need to look around."

When she nodded, he glanced around at the crowd of men and motioned for Jason to come forward and sit with her. "Stay close and don't let anyone near her."

Jason nodded, his eyes heavy with concern. As Hunter walked away, he heard Jason offer to pray with Tabitha, and though he didn't hear her reply, the older man's prayer immediately filled the air.

The other men drifted off, and Hunter scoured the area around the tent. He found no sign of anyone lurking around, though he hadn't expected the culprit to wait for him. He'd brought the lantern along and saw a dark shadow of a figure walking toward him.

Lifting the lantern, he called ahead, "Who's out there?"

"It's me, Mr. Pierce, Joey Matthews. Will you kindly stop bellowing?" Joey's voice, though always put out, sounded more stressed than usual. "What's going on over here?"

"Someone sneaked into Miss Augustine's tent and threatened her."

Joey had reached the circle of light and stopped short of it. Did he have something to hide? Hunter watched carefully for any signs of something being out of order.

"This is exactly why she needs to leave."

"Interesting. Those are more or less the words her intruder stated."

"Are you accusing me?"

Hunter stepped closer and lifted the lantern so he could see Joey's face. "I don't know. Should I be?"

Joey squinted into the brightness. "Get that thing out of my face."

Hunter lowered the lantern a bit but didn't move away. "You haven't answered my question. Do you know anything about the intruder or what happened in her tent tonight?"

Joey wouldn't look him in the eye. "I don't know what you're talking about, but if someone told her to leave, they have more sense than she does. She needs to heed the warning and go."

"That sounds like a threat to me. Where were you when

everyone else came running? I find it interesting that you're arriving now, after the fact."

"That's none of your business. I don't have to answer to you." Joey glared. "And you'd do well to mind your own business."

Hunter turned his back on the man and ignored his last words. He walked back to Tabitha and relieved Jason of his guard duty. The man muttered something about keeping her in his prayers and hobbled back toward his site.

"You need to go inside and try to get some more sleep."

"How can I do that? I'm sure I'll not sleep a wink now that I've been accosted."

She had a point. Hunter surveyed her site and then his. "I tell you what. I'll sit outside here and doze in my chair. Nothing will get past me. We'll sort this out in the morning."

He helped her to her feet and gave her a gentle shove in the direction of her tent. "Secure it tightly after you go inside. You'll be fine."

If Hunter had to stay awake the rest of the night, he'd make sure of it.

ਏ

Morning came quicker than Tabitha wanted, but she'd been able to sleep in sporadic stretches. When she stepped out from her tent, she was surprised to see several gaps where tents were missing from various sites.

"They packed up during the night and moved out at first light," Hunter called over to her. He sat on a crate outside his own tent and worked on his broken sledgehammer. "It seems as though someone's threatening the other archaeologists, too."

While Tabitha supposed she should feel relief at Hunter's

words, she only felt a pang of apprehension. What was going on?

"Is Mr. Matthews going to do something about this? It seems it's his place to make sure the process is carried out with integrity."

Hunter walked toward her and propped his foot up on a box. "I'm not sure. You'd think so, but he's not spoken to anyone, nor have I seen him today."

A thin sheen of dust had coated the chair, and she stooped to wipe it off. "The rain sure didn't make a difference in the dryness around here."

"No, it usually doesn't." Hunter grinned. "The rain soaks into the ground, and an hour later there's no sign it ever happened."

"I guess it's a good thing since we need to continue working. Digging in mud would surely cause problems."

"How are you feeling today? Do you have any lasting effects from last night?"

"Such as?" She was sore. Her arm hurt. She'd had nightmare after nightmare. But she doubted Hunter really cared to hear all that.

"How's your arm?"

"Sore."

"Did you sleep?"

"A bit." She grinned.

"You find something about my questions amusing."

The comment was more statement than question. "I didn't figure you'd be interested in such detail."

"I'd not have asked if I wasn't interested. I don't waste words."

"I've noticed."

They returned to their companionable silence. The camp came alive as other scientists emerged from their tents and headed over to the eating area. Neither made an attempt to join them until Tabitha shot to her feet.

"I have an idea."

Hunter stood next to her, watching the diners in the next section, and folded his arms. "What's that?"

"Well, if we're all being threatened one by one, and someone is determined to chase us off from reaching our dream and being part of this history-making event, why don't we all band together as a group?"

"The idea has merit. How do you propose we go about this?"

Appreciation of her suggestion filled Hunter's eyes, and Tabitha felt her heart skip a beat.

"Well, for starters, we can join the men eating over there and see what we come up with together."

"You amaze me, Tabitha Augustine. Most women would have left long ago, but you're figuring out a battle plan. I'm proud of you."

"Thanks." Tabitha turned away so Hunter couldn't see the effect his words had on her heart. A higher compliment, she couldn't imagine.

ঽ

Hunter watched in amazement as Tabitha united the remaining men into a watch group. Over the past few weeks, she had evolved from a harsh but insecure woman to a gentle and independent one. The men had gone from resenting her to pretending she didn't exist to embracing her and her ideas.

Though he respected her desire to stay and her determination to see this through, he knew it would be best for her to return to her father's care and to leave the dangerous situation they now found themselves in.

Convincing her would be the hard part. He contemplated how to approach her with his thought as they worked. After dinner, Tabitha excused herself for a bit and went into her tent.

He'd missed his chance. The evening stretched before him, and he wished Tab would come out and enjoy the summer sunset with him. Though the bluffs blocked their view of the actual event, the sky would light up with glorious colors as the fiery ball dipped low beyond the horizon. Hunter's next thought was to wonder where the previous crazy thought had come from. He blamed it on his lack of sleep. He'd never needed anyone else in his life before and didn't need anyone now. He and the good Lord had done just fine without throwing in a woman's interfering ways, especially a woman who hadn't embraced the Lord in the same way as he had.

He waited a bit to see if she'd return, but when she didn't, he headed over to her tent, knowing he needed to tell her how he felt. As soon as he arrived, he rethought his idea, deciding it could wait.

Just as he turned to walk away, he heard her quiet voice. "Oh no."

A moment's hesitation and then, "This can't be."

Her anguish was palpable.

"Tab? What is it?" His heart pounded at the thought that someone had again attacked her in her tent, under his watch. He fought the urge to burst into the tent uninvited.

"Hunter. . ." Her voice tapered off as she stepped outside. Her tears again flowed freely. "I needed to go through my father's trunk, and I found this note. I can't believe what he's done."

She held it out, and his eyes widened in question. He wondered how he'd originally missed the fact that she was such a delicate and dainty woman. And at times like this, her vulnerability completely overshadowed her academic role.

"Read it. Please." She pushed a stray blond strand of hair behind her ear.

Hunter took the proffered piece of paper and glanced at it. As he skimmed the first few words, he slowed down and began to read more carefully. "It's a statement of some kind."

"Yes."

"I'm not sure I understand."

"My father apparently gave up his chance for the win for a very large sum of money."

"Why would he do this?" Hunter searched for an explanation. "Someone must have been very confident in your father's skills to offer such an amount to get rid of him."

"Well, besides the recognition and hoopla for the actual find, you know there'll be more to it than that. The winner will assist with the actual dig and will surely be offered worldwide opportunities to speak of the experience. The long-term financial effect could be far-reaching."

"Hmm. I've not thought it through that much. I just enjoy the quest. And I enjoy touching history."

"But it won't end there for you or anyone else who wins."

"I'm starting to realize that."

The situation increased his concern for her safety, but he decided that instead of rushing to approach her about leaving, he'd be better off praying about the whole situation. "What do you plan to do?"

"I have no choice. I'll leave first thing in the morning and go into town to talk this over with my father. I plan to return by nightfall or the day after tomorrow at the latest."

Hunter felt relief at her words. He'd pray she would see the practicality of staying in town with her father and that this turn of events would show her the need to turn her life over to God. He couldn't imagine going through life without the guidance his faith offered him, but especially in times like this, he desired and was drawn close to the One who watched over him.

He realized how lonely Tabitha must be with neither her earthly father nor the heavenly Father to lean on. He prayed that God would wrap her in His protection as she traveled and that no more dangerous events would threaten her safety while she was away from him. He knew he'd offer to accompany her on the trek because no treasure or find was more important than her safety. But he also knew that with her stubborn streak, the offer would most likely be declined. He couldn't force her to take him along. Instead, he would continue to trust and pray for her safety.

ten

Tab arranged for a ride into town on the supply wagon and glanced around at the landscape as they entered Vernal. Horse-drawn wagons hurried along both sides of the street, people bustled about, and all the activity felt foreign after her stay at the dig site. The trip to town had been uneventful, but the more they'd traveled, the more she realized how gritty she felt and how much a part of her life the grubby feeling had become. Now, as she watched the womenfolk walk from store to store in all their finery, she suddenly realized she had one goal more important than that of talking to her father. She wanted—no, she needed—to find the closest hotel where she could reserve a room and have a hot bath. For this one day she'd feel clean and dress in the frilly, feminine dress she'd brought along.

The wagon master assisted her to the ground in front of the general store and handed her the satchel he'd lifted from behind the seat. After procuring directions from the shopkeeper to the lone hotel, she walked briskly toward the worn building. The town's noise filled her ears, and she hoped the hotel would be a nice buffer from the chaos that filled the streets and walkways outside.

Though its door stood open to the elements, she let out a sigh of relief at the muffled quiet that surrounded her as she walked into the posh setting. Thick carpet covered the floor, and floral wall covering gave the entry area a cozy feel. The woman behind the desk sent her a warm smile, and Tabitha hurried over to the counter.

"What can I do for you?" The middle-aged woman motioned for her to set her satchel down.

Tabitha did so with relief. "I need a room and hopefully a hot bath."

"We can take care of that. How many nights will you be staying?"

"Just this one. Could you tell me if my father has checked into this establishment? His name is Peter Augustine."

The woman's face lit up as she registered Tabitha's comment. "You're Dr. Augustine's daughter? Oh, we're so glad to have you here. Peter has told me all about you." She hurried around the long counter, and Tabitha found herself in a tight embrace from the older woman.

"So you do know of him?" Tabitha knew her comment was redundant, and with the woman's obvious familiarity with Tab's father, speaking of him by his first name, she surely knew of him.

"Oh my, yes." The woman actually blushed. "Peter has stayed here from the first moment he stepped foot in town two weeks ago. He's been very worried and, as a matter of fact, planned to leave first thing tomorrow to travel out and check up on you."

"Well, now that I'm here, he won't need to take the trip. I'm glad we didn't cross paths and miss each other." Tabitha found herself warming to the woman.

"Oh my, where are my manners? My name is Bitsy. Bitsy Barnes. I'm going to set you up in one of our most comfortable rooms, and I'll have your bath drawn immediately. As soon as I have that taken care of, I'll notify your father of your arrival.

He's going to be so happy to know you're here safe and sound."

Not after he finds out why I've come. Tabitha kept her thoughts to herself, nodded her agreement, and followed Bitsy up the carpeted stairway and down a long hall. They stopped outside a room at the far end while Bitsy worked a key into the lock.

"You'll have a corner room and views of two different streets down below." Bitsy hurried over to the window and pulled back the curtains. A soft breeze blew through the room. "Your father's room is just across the hall, but he's not in at the moment. He'll be back shortly for dinner, and you two can catch up then. I'll tell him to meet you down in the dining room, that is, if that suits you."

"Yes, thank you. That will be fine."

"I'm sorry. I tend to be a tad bossy. You be sure to tell me if I'm overstepping."

This time Tabitha smiled. She could grow to like Bitsy and wondered if her father had finally met his match. "I'll be sure to do just that, but for now I'm fine with all that you've suggested."

"Then I'll leave you to your bath." Bitsy motioned for her assistant to bring the tub in. "I'll send some water up immediately. Enjoy."

Tabitha surely would. The thought of feeling clean, if only for a day, drew her like no other.

❧

Clean and freshly dressed, Tabitha hurried down to dinner. She'd twisted her hair into an elaborate style that complimented her light blue dress. As she reached the entrance to the dining room, she hesitated, seeking out the table where her father waited. It didn't take long to find him. His face lit up at the sight of her, and Tabitha hurried over to him as he stood.

"You look beautiful," her father said after giving her a quick hug. He pulled out the padded chair opposite him for her, and she sat down. "I'm so glad you've finally come to your senses and decided to join me here."

Tabitha couldn't believe how heavenly a proper chair felt. The rough-hewn seats at the tables on the dig site were incredibly hard and uncomfortable, almost as uncomfortable as Tabitha felt at her father's words.

"I've not come to stay. I'm only here for the night. I'll catch the supply wagon back to the site tomorrow at daybreak."

She didn't miss the disappointment that swept across his face. She felt bad that her words caused a sudden rift to return between them that moments earlier had been gone.

A young girl hurried over to take their order. Her father suggested the daily special, and Tabitha nodded her agreement. Their server hurried off toward the kitchen where savory scents wafted through the door.

Tabitha found herself wishing they could enjoy the meal before she got to the point of her visit, but she knew her father was never one to mince words and didn't like others to do so, either.

She glanced down at her distorted reflection in the silverware and tried to figure out the wording of what she needed to ask. There was no good way to ask someone why they'd sold out on their dreams.

"I found a note in the tent." She glanced up at her father, and he returned her look, perplexed.

"A note? And this note caused you to take a day's trip into town? What note?"

She stayed silent and watched as several emotions crossed

his face. Confusion. Awareness. Dismay. He began to shake his head in denial, even as she spoke.

"Please don't speak of this."

"Father, the note offered you a large sum of money for pulling out of the dig! Why would you ever consider doing such a thing? This has never been about the money for us."

Suddenly her father's face held all the emotion of a poker player. A well-practiced poker player. "You shouldn't have read the note, and I'll not explain my actions to you."

Tabitha slapped her hand down on the tabletop, causing several people to look their way. She hurried to control her own emotions before returning her eyes to her father. "You've shut me out ever since we've arrived. It's because of that note, isn't it? You dragged me all the way out here and never even intended for us to stay. Why?"

He wilted before her eyes. "I didn't come out here intending to quit. I've wanted this for a long time. You know that. But after I started to get the threats and things escalated, I decided that for both of our good, it would be best if we accepted the money and left."

"But *we* didn't accept the money, Papa, *you* did. I knew nothing about it. Don't you think for my own safety the least you could have done was tell me what I faced? Did you not think I had any interest in this?"

"I thought you'd leave with me, and after you refused, I figured if I pulled out, the mishaps would stop because no one would take you seriously."

"Well, the mishaps haven't stopped. If anything, they've escalated." Tabitha forced herself to stop there, without detail. It wouldn't do any good to get her father more riled up. He'd forbid her to return, and that was a chance she couldn't take.

"I feel safe for now, and Hunter is watching over me, just as he promised, but others have been forced out. You should have confided in me and trusted that I could be a part of your decision. I miss you."

"I miss you, too, but this decision was mine alone to make and didn't concern you. I don't think you need to continue the work out there after this, either. We're set financially and can go back East and settle down. You can focus on finding a husband—if it's not already too late. I've made a mistake in dragging you around all these years, and we need to remedy that."

Tabitha shot to her feet. "There's nothing to remedy. I've enjoyed our life and wouldn't change a thing. And it's been my decision along with yours. If you want to make such a decision for yourself, I know I can't change your mind. But I will be returning to the dig, and I will see this through to the end. I will not sit by while a manipulative criminal chases everyone away in the name of money." Tabitha spun on her heels and hurried from the room, ignoring her father's call from behind.

Bitsy stood behind the counter, her face creased with concern. "Oh dear. I'd hoped your visit would be a good one and we could perhaps get to know each other a bit better."

Tabitha slowed and let go of some of her anger. "Maybe another time. For now, if you don't mind, I'll have my dinner in my room." She needed to be alone to figure out her next move and couldn't return to the dig site fast enough.

❧

"He didn't have any good reason for selling out?" Hunter's concern after her return the next day lifted the first layer of sadness her father's harsh reaction had brought on. He watched as her face registered surprise that he'd care. He stood outside her tent, arms crossed at his chest, feeling very ferocious and protective.

Tabitha shook her head. "Not any reason I consider good enough. He said the money would allow us to move back East and settle down. He wants me to find a. . ." She allowed her voice to trail off as a charming flush settled over her features. "Never mind."

"Find a what?" Hunter loved to tease Tab when she set herself up in such a way.

Tabitha looked at the bluff and refused to meet his eyes. "A husband. All right? He wants me to find a husband."

Suddenly Hunter didn't feel so cocky. The notion of Tabitha taking a husband, with said husband not being him, didn't sit too well.

She glanced back at him and this time stared straight into his eyes. "But I'm not interested."

He had a momentary panic that she'd read his thoughts. "Not interested?"

"I've met plenty of men," she continued, "and not one has ever caught my eye in such a way that'd I'd choose to spend the rest of my life settled down and stuck in one place with him."

Hunter, feeling brave, moved a step closer. "Not a one? No potential husband has ever turned your head? Not even me?" He had no idea where those words had come from.

"Oh stop. You're only trying to make me blush. I've no need for another male in my life. My father's quite enough to handle, thank you very much."

"Well, I hate to be the one to inform you—oh, not really, I rather enjoy being the one to inform you—but you're already blushing. And whoever said marriage meant you'd have to settle down? I can promise you that if you were to marry me, we'd be anything but settled."

"Hunter, if that's a proposal, it's the worst one I've ever heard."

He now wondered if she'd heard a lot of them. He had to admit that by being constantly surrounded by men with the life she led, he'd be a fool to believe no other male had ever noticed her quiet beauty, let alone asked for her hand in marriage. She probably left a trail of more broken hearts in ports throughout the world than any sailor he'd ever met. The thought saddened him. He didn't want to be one of many in a long line of Tabitha-caused broken hearts.

Tabitha stared at him more closely. "You were joking, weren't you?"

"Would it be so awful if I were serious? You're a beautiful woman, Tab, and I've come to enjoy your company."

"Thank you." Hunter had to lean in to hear her quiet words. "No one's ever told me that before."

"I mean it. Though I never thought I'd say them back when we met. You didn't come across as the same woman you are now."

Tilting her head, Tabitha considered his statement. "I believe you're right. I am different now. With my father away, a new side of me has emerged. And I have to admit, I kind of like the Tabitha I've become."

&

"I like the Tabitha you've become, too. And I liked the Tabitha you were. Don't leave her behind." Hunter's grin charmed her.

Hunter continued to hold her attention as he searched for his next words. "You know you don't have to be alone anymore, either, right? Even with your father gone?"

"Is this another marriage proposal?" Tabitha laughed.

The thought actually intrigued her, and she'd found herself fantasizing of late about what life would be like with Hunter as her husband. She knew there would never be a dull moment, for one thing. But this was a perfect example of how she had changed now that her father no longer stood around to censor her thoughts with his constant focus on work or how she should believe and act.

Never before had she even considered marriage, let alone had her thoughts run wild with dreams of marriage to a certain man. Now that they'd had this conversation, she realized she was lonely and only a husband would fill the void in her desire for a life companion. Her father's company was nice, but he tended to lecture and teach. They had no give and take, nor a friendship of any sort. She longed for a friend—and more—and Hunter was the friend she wanted. Her life would be incredibly empty after they went their separate ways, a situation she didn't even want to think about.

She realized as her mind drifted and pondered her future, Hunter was answering her question about marriage, which she first thought she'd thrown out in jest, but now realized was a true desire of her heart.

"Not exactly a marriage proposal. I guess you'd say it was more of a 'you have a heavenly Father just waiting for you to acknowledge Him' proposal."

Tabitha felt a mixture of emotions at his comment. Embarrassment that she'd misread him. Disappointment that he apparently didn't share her dreams about a shared marriage in their near future. And frustration and irritation that he never gave up and once again pushed her toward God. That frustration made her words come out more harshly than she intended.

"Hunter, if you want to believe, it's a choice you're free to make. But as I've told you before, I'm not ready to make a decision about something like that. Someday, when life slows down, I'll research all angles thoroughly, but until then, I have too many scholastic pursuits that override my desire to worry about studies of the unknown."

"But they're not unknown." Hunter let out an exasperated breath. "The Bible is very clear."

"And reputable scholars will refute you with the fact that the Bible is fiction."

"The Bible is absolutely *not* fiction." A vein at the side of Hunter's neck now throbbed with his intensity. "I'll not remain here and listen to you say such a thing. You can disagree with my stance and beliefs, but I'll not stand by while you blaspheme the Word."

"Hunter, don't be angry," Tabitha softened her voice. "I only said there are scholars who would argue with you. I didn't say I was one of them. You need to give me leniency and time. I've told you, my father taught me early on to believe only what could be seen and proven, not the things that cannot be seen and cannot be proven. I have agreed to be open, but you keep pushing your beliefs at me."

"I've pushed nothing. I've only spoken the truth. Hebrews 11:1 states, 'Now faith is the substance of things hoped for, the evidence of things not seen.' This is completely opposite of what your father has taught you. Maybe you need to expand your horizons and realize there's more out there than what your father has wanted you to see. I sure don't see him standing here beside you fighting for what's right. If you don't want to listen to me, you have that choice." Hunter stated his words carefully. "But, Tabitha, sometimes your time runs out, and it's too late to make a decision about Christ. You have someone after you out here. You can't deny that. If this person, even under my watchful eye, catches either one of us by surprise and something happens to you, it will be too late. And I'll have that on my soul for the rest of my life."

With that last comment, he turned and walked away toward his camp.

Tabitha stomped her foot and growled with frustration. His words repeated over and over in her mind. She wasn't a child to take only her father's teachings to heart and no others, but he had taught her to use her own mind to make decisions and not just take someone else's words for granted. But was that what she'd done? In all honesty, she had to wonder.

Tired from her long day, she stepped into her tent and prepared for bed. She pulled a nightgown over her head and slipped under her cool sheet. She'd analyze things as she waited for sleep to claim her. She had a feeling that even as tired as she was, sleep would prove to be elusive. Hunter's words had struck a chord deep inside, and though she didn't want to think poorly of her father, she had to admit that though he stated one thing—that she needed to be free to search out her own truth—her father did have a way of guiding her to his truth and thoughts and beliefs.

"I don't see how God has anything to do with my disappointments or my father's choice to sell out," she muttered into the darkness. Her granny's face floated through her consciousness, and Tabitha had such a sudden homesickness for the woman, it cut her to the core. She missed her. And she realized the best thing she could do to feel close to her granny would be to read the Bible that was so dear to the woman's heart. She'd promised Hunter she'd read it but had let her reading time go of late with all that had gone on. Since her whirlwind thoughts kept sleep at bay, she sat up and reached over to light her lamp. She pulled the Bible from her trunk and opened it to the verse Hunter had quoted. As she read, another sense of peace passed through her, just as it had when Hunter had prayed. With the turmoil that had been at the forefront of her mind for the past few days, that unexplainable emotion alone showed she was on the right track.

❧

Hunter saw Tabitha's lantern come on and hurried over to her tent. "Tab? Is everything okay?"

"I'm fine, Hunter. I couldn't sleep so am doing a bit of research." Tabitha's calm voice through the fabric of her tent brought him a measure of peace.

"All right. I just wanted to be sure." He stood silently, hoping she'd say she needed to talk. Those words never came.

The camp was mostly quiet at this hour, the majority of men sleeping after a hard day of digging. He grinned at the snores that carried to him on the night breeze. Such a sound must constantly remind Tabitha that she lived in a man's world. He could hear muffled voices here and there as a few night owls sat around a fire. A lone man walked toward the end of the road where the outhouse sat silhouetted under the full moon. Dark fluffy clouds momentarily obscured the illuminating orb, only to move quickly by, allowing light to reach back over the camp.

"Thank you for checking on me." She hesitated a moment. "And thank you for caring."

"I'll always care, Tab." His hand reached for the cloth that separated them, but he didn't allow himself to make contact.

"I don't want you upset with me, but I have to share what I consider to be most dear to my heart. I'll try not to push so hard in the future."

Her sweet sigh carried through the night air and brought another smile to Hunter's lips. "Don't hold back from me, Hunter. I want to know your heart."

"Well, if you're sure." Silence filled a few more moments. "I'll be off to my tent then. Call if you need me."

"I will. G'night."

"Good night."

She's not angry at me. The thought filled him with more relief than it should. He'd tried not to care, not in the way his heart had begun to long for. Without a shared faith, he couldn't move further into a relationship with the woman he now knew he loved.

He only wished he could better share what his faith meant to him and the peace in all situations he drew from the knowledge that there was more at work in his life than random happenings that were out of his control. With his concern for Tabitha the past few weeks, he'd grown away from that security. If only the woman he loved shared his beliefs, he'd be able to pray with her consistently and things wouldn't feel as out of control as they now did.

He could remedy his own lack of action by getting back to the Word and focusing more on prayer. His first prayer would be for Tabitha to understand. His second would be for her safety. She might not be open to God at the moment, but his faith alone would fill the gap, and he'd pray for her until he could convince her of God's love and direction for her life.

If Tabitha would only acknowledge God, she could use her trust of Him to carry her through this dangerous and confusing time. Instead, she leaned on her own under-standing, and he had no way to comfort her. Her quest overruled the urgency of her finding God. Hunter's hate of riches and prestige flared, taking him by surprise. Her father should have stayed, and he should be the one to worry about and watch over her. Instead, he'd gone for the money and left her behind.

Hunter had grown up with everything he could ever want, but until his good friend told him about the Lord, he never felt truly happy. Now, after learning the truth of what life was really about and what he needed to focus on, he preferred to live without excess money. Tab's father's decision to throw everything he'd lived for away—to give up his dreams for a bit of money—reinforced that thought.

Money might not be the cause of all evil, but he could see how the love of money did indeed allow evil to carry on.

eleven

Tabitha pushed herself up from her cot early the next morning after lifting the heavy Bible off her chest. She'd apparently gone to sleep in the wee hours after reading too many of the pages. Instead of feeling tired, though, she felt refreshed. The words the book contained brought a gentle quiet to her restless heart, and she now knew what she had to do.

She hurried to dress so she could find Hunter and share her thoughts. He'd be happy to hear that she'd followed through on her promise to stay open to God's Word and her spirit felt renewed from her reading.

"Good morning, Hunter!" She hurried to where he squatted over a box at his site, making him jump at her sudden arrival. "Sorry."

She couldn't hide her giggle at his reaction, and a slow grin filled his features as he stood to look down at her.

"Good morning." He wiped the dust from his hands onto an old rag before stuffing it back into his pocket. "You seem to be in a good mood today. What's the occasion?"

"A woman has to have a reason to be in a good mood?" Tabitha surveyed his site, putting her plan into motion as they bantered about with small talk. At a lull in their conversation, she said, "I have an idea."

"Ah, so here comes the reason. I knew there was a catch."

His smile caused her heart to skip a beat. He really was a handsome man. "Um. . ." She couldn't remember what they were talking about. His nearness suddenly did strange things to her mind. Her thoughts scattered in all directions. "What were we talking about?"

"I believe you were getting ready to tell me how you planned to stage my day." His warm laughter filled her heart. She wanted to hear the sound again and again. This phase of their relationship surely beat the first few weeks when they always found themselves at each other's throat.

Tab sighed. "I'm not about to 'stage your day.' I merely have a new direction I think we should go. . . ."

"We?"

She felt the flush cover her cheeks as she stumbled over her own words. She'd been watching his hair blow in the wind. Her mind again drifted to thoughts of their future, a future he obviously wanted to tease her about but that her mind wanted to grab on to with all the possibilities.

"Oh, uh, we, as in, the team, you and I. The dig team, that is. Where we both work together to find those elusive bones." She huffed. "Oh bother! I can't seem to think."

Hunter leaned against his shovel and stared at her in a most disarming way. The forward movement brought his face nearer her own, and she caught her breath as his warm brown eyes drifted down to her mouth. She glanced at his full lips and irrationally wished he'd kissed her while they were up on the bluff. Though she wasn't as wise to the ways of the world as she knew many other women must be, she did know Hunter had come close to kissing her while they sat in that remote place. And she also knew that with him being the respectful man that he was in such a private place, he'd never dishonor her by kissing her here, in full view of the entire camp.

"I think you were about to plan our day." After another

long, measured glance, he abruptly stood up straight and walked a few feet away, putting space between them.

Tabitha decided it would be more fun to show him what she'd planned. She hurried to the crate farthest away from his tent, the one that rested against the rock wall. She rummaged around inside it and triumphantly pulled out what she'd been looking for.

"Tab. . .what are you doing?" Hunter looked perplexed.

She hurried over to the place where Hunter had blown out the hole in the wall. "Help me out here."

Hunter let loose a strangled sound and hurried to her side. "What are you thinking? Give me that."

He pulled the dynamite gently from her hands. "This stuff is very sensitive and dangerous." After setting it aside, he pulled her by the hands and led her over to sit on a different crate from the one she'd found the dynamite in. "Now tell me what you're thinking."

"I can't sit here any longer and sift through miniscule amounts of dust. I want to find the bones. I want to show my father we can win this and that there's more to life than money. I want. . ." Much to her embarrassment, her voice cracked and tears spilled from her eyes. "I want my life to be as it was."

Hunter pulled her into his warm embrace, not seeming to care what the others around them might think. "I know, sweetheart. This hasn't exactly been the experience I expected it to be, either." He caressed her back, the movement the most wonderful sensation she'd ever felt.

"I'm sorry. I know what you mean. I've been nothing but trouble to you." Her words and sobs were muffled by his shirtfront.

"Nah, that's not what I meant at all. Look at me." He

gently lifted her chin, forcing her to look into his eyes. "The distraction of you is the most wonderful thing I've ever found on a dig."

"Really?" Her heart began to beat double time again at his words, but the look in his eyes made her want to swoon. Only the knowledge that a swoon would pull her out of this moment held her together.

"Really." His voice had dropped to a husky whisper. He dropped his hand from her chin and took her hands in both of his. "Listen, Tabitha. I know things haven't been easy. And I know this experience hasn't been what you expected. But I'm here to help you through it. We are going to get through it. I promise."

She could do nothing at the moment except nod.

"I'm sure your father had a reason for his decision, and I'm sorry it hurt you, but we can move forward as you've planned, and we can make the most of things as they are." His fingers absently caressed the back of her hands. "What do you think?"

She couldn't actually think much at all past the fact that he held her hands so securely with his and that his caresses muddled every intelligent thought in her head. "I, uh, I think you're right."

Those words were certainly less than intelligent. She cringed and rolled her eyes. Hunter let loose another heartfelt laugh, and she felt her mouth quirk up in response.

"I hate money."

Hunter pulled her to her feet. "So do I, Tab, so do I."

⋆

Tabitha led him over to the rock wall and pointed to the dynamite he'd carefully set aside. "Let's do it."

"Excuse me?"

"The dynamite. Let's blow through this rock and see what's hiding behind it."

Hunter cocked his hand to his ear. "I'm sorry. One more time, please? I'm afraid I must not be hearing very well this morning. I do believe that you, Miss Scratch-the-surface-off-the-dirt-below-us, just suggested that we blast our way through the precious bluff that protects the ancient secrets of the past."

"Yes, well, the previous blast of dynamite from your early days here surely did damage your hearing if you can't follow the simple and direct words I'm saying. But I did suggest just such a thing. I'm tired of playing it safe."

He watched in amazement as the prim and proper strait-laced woman from a few weeks before stood before him and spun in a circle with her arms spread wide toward the heavens. The smile on her face as she tilted it skyward with eyes closed in a moment of pure abandonment had him smiling in response. She was breathtakingly beautiful.

As she stopped her spinning and stood and surveyed him with a goofy grin on her face, he stepped toward her.

"Tab?"

"What?"

"Let's blow this mountain."

"Yes, let's."

They hurried to the wall of sandstone, and Hunter showed her how to place the dynamite for the best blast and least amount of damage to the underlying fossils. He then sent her across to her own site—though they'd taken down the rope that had previously outlined their separate spaces—where she could watch in safety. He ran to join her as the blast rocked their area. He pulled her into a protective embrace as dust and small fragments of rock fell around them.

This time, instead of berating him as she had the last time he'd used this method, she threw back her head and laughed with merriment as the men stationed near their site stumbled from their tents while attempting to force their legs into their clothing.

"I'm so sorry," she laughed into her hand, not sounding the least bit sorry at all.

The other men must have realized the same thing, because instead of grumping about the abrupt wake-up, they exchanged amused smiles as they watched Tabitha's uninhibited glee.

"C'mon, let's see what we've uncovered." Tabitha tugged at Hunter's hand and led him toward the wall. As they neared the freshly blown spot, she dropped his hand and hurried forward to inspect the area they'd uncovered.

Jason walked up and hooked his fingers through his suspenders. "I don't know what you been doin' to that girl, but whatever it is, keep it up." He shook his head in a way that had his wild gray hair flying. "She's a balm to my heart when she lets loose like this."

"I don't know that I did anything to change her," Hunter defended with a shake of his head. He turned and grinned at the old man. "But if I ever figure out the secret, I'll surely use it again."

"Oh, I think you know the secret." Jason looked at him with knowing eyes. "The woman is in love."

"Now wait just a minute." Hunter glanced around to make sure no one else heard the man's crazy words. "It's nothing like that, I'm sure. I think she's just needed to get a breather from her father's overbearing ways, and I'm the one nearby she's found to be a safe place."

"Mm-hmm. If you say so." Jason sent him another knowing look and turned to walk away. "Just make sure you don't bungle things up for the rest of us. We're enjoying her fun-loving nature and can't wait to see what she has in store for us next."

Hunter watched the man walk away and shook his head. Who'd have thought him to be such a romantic? He returned his attention to Tabitha, who now brushed the last of the dust away and turned to him with dismay.

"There aren't any bones."

"Really? Well, then, let's get busy and blow some more of this bluff out of our way."

&

Tabitha stepped backward as more rock sailed her way. Tiny pieces fell around her, but she wasn't concerned. Hunter's skill enabled him to set the blast in such a way as not to put them in a harmful situation. So far their more aggressive approach hadn't moved their search forward. As Tabitha waited for the dust to die down, a sharp pain pierced her upper arm, and she cried out in response.

"Ah." She ducked her head and fell to her knees, clutching her arm tightly with her other hand. She gasped for breath and laid her head down on her upper legs as the burning pain intensified. She rasped out the first name that came to mind. "Hunter."

When he didn't appear at her side, she forced her head up and tried to see him through her tears. "Oh, Hunter. It hurts. I need you." Her words were barely a whisper, and she knew there was no way he could hear her.

A piece of rock must have ricocheted off the cliffs and

nicked her arm. Her head spun as she tried to see the damage. Blood coated the torn sleeve of her blouse and spread to soak into the fabric across her chest, the sight causing her stomach to turn in horror.

"Tabitha!" Hunter's voice carried to her from far away. "Sweetheart, what happened?"

She heard footsteps pound the ground and could hear his voice, but it seemed to come from far away. No words came forth as she tried to answer. She heard the anguish as he yelled for help, his tone one she'd never heard before, just before everything went hazy.

"Tabitha. Please, honey, answer me."

Pain continued to shoot through Tab's arm, and she fought consciousness. Though she felt his gentle, rhythmic caress on her hand, she refused to do as he asked. It hurt too much. She'd rather go back to that dark place.

He pushed her hair from her face as he told everyone to move away and give her some space. Grumblings showed the men didn't want to leave, but their footfalls receded.

She gave in to the haziness and drifted away.

❧

"Tabitha, c'mon. You need to wake up." Hunter didn't care who heard the emotion in his voice. "Come on, please. I need you to wake up. I need you. Tabby, please."

"Hunter. Shush. I'm not a cat."

Hunter sat back on his heels and thanked God she'd finally responded. Even though her voice sounded disgruntled and the barb was aimed in his direction, he hadn't ever heard more wonderful words in his entire life.

"How do you feel?"

"Like the entire mountain collapsed on one small spot of

my arm. It's throbbing, but not as much as before."

She'd not yet opened her eyes. He worried that she'd also taken a blow to the head—perhaps they'd overlooked it in all the chaos.

He felt the panic well up and tried to control the shaking of his voice. "Tabitha, can you see? Open your eyes."

"I got hit in the arm by a rock, Hunter, not in the head." She turned and blinked at him, her blue eyes staring up at him with reproach.

"You were shot, Tab. You weren't struck by a rock."

He watched her glance around, taking in the fact that she rested on her cot in her tent. "But how. . . ?"

"I'd guess from the trajectory—based on the path from which the bullet entered and exited your arm and how you were standing when shot—that the coward once again stood up on the bluff. The same place where he pushed the boulder down."

She let her eyes drift closed. "I wish we'd blown him clean off the face of the cliff with our dynamite."

"Tabitha!"

Hunter found it encouraging that she had the ability to smirk through her pain, even if she didn't reopen her eyes.

"Well, maybe not clean off the face, but maybe backward enough so he'd feel a bit of the pain I'm feeling right about now."

"We gave you some medicine to help. Isn't it working?" Hunter couldn't stand it if she felt severe pain.

"It's helping some. I feel much better than I did." She opened her eyes and glanced at him again. "How long have I been out?"

"A few hours."

"Oh."

He fussed with the sheet that covered her.

"I feel much better than I did a few hours ago then."

The doctor pushed his way through the opening of the tent. Jason stood from where he'd been keeping watch so no one would talk about improprieties. Hunter started to argue when the doctor motioned him out, too.

"I hear our patient has finally come around." When Hunter hesitated at the tent's opening, the doctor motioned him forward. "I'll fill you in as soon as I have a look at her. She's going to be fine, Hunter."

"Doc, if it's all the same to you, I'd like for Hunter to stay."

Hunter's heart danced at Tabitha's words. She wanted him to stay. He just about busted a button on his shirt over the pride her words evoked.

"Very well, but stay back."

Hunter moved to the end of the cot and placed a reassuring hand upon Tabitha's foot. It felt delicate through the thin fabric of her sheet.

The doctor examined Tabitha's eyes and then pulled the bandages from her wound. Hunter had been so upset when the attack happened that he'd focused on keeping Tabitha awake more than on what the doctor had discovered. Now he felt his anger burst forth at the ugly wound that sliced down her arm.

"Ouch!" Tabitha jerked and her foot slipped away from Hunter's hand.

"I'm sorry," Doc said with remorse, momentarily releasing his grip on her arm. "Did I hit a tender spot? I'm trying to keep my hand away from the sore area. Maybe we missed something?"

"No, you're doing fine. Hunter just about squeezed the life out of my foot, though."

"Sorry." Hunter flinched. "But I hadn't seen the wound before now. I want to get my hands around the man's neck who did this to you."

"Spoken like a true man of God." Tabitha smirked.

Hunter shook his head at her amusement. "So maybe that isn't exactly the response God would want from me, but I'm only human. I know I need to turn the anger over to Him, but I'd give about anything right now to help Him in doling out punishment."

"He won't need help from what you've told me. Don't let bitterness creep in on my account, Hunter."

"Yes, ma'am." He waited for her to open her eyes and meet his. "Tab. You know you need to leave now. The shooter might not miss next time. Remember what we talked about the other night? That sometimes things happen and it's too late to make things right with God? This almost became that time."

"I know, Hunter, and I've given it a lot of thought since then. I want to talk more about it. But if you send me away, that talk will never happen."

She had his attention with that comment, he had to admit.

"And I doubt the rough trip would be good for me in my condition, right, Doc?"

"Don't pull me into your squabble," Doc stated without missing a step of his examination. He'd tended to her wound and now wrapped a fresh piece of cloth around her arm. "I'd say Tabitha would be the best judge of her ability to travel."

"And I judge that the trip would be too difficult for me at this time," Tabitha insisted. Her stubbornness had reached a new level.

"The pain will be intense for at least the next few days and will still be annoying you for quite a while thereafter. I'll leave some more medications in case the pain intensifies over the next day or so."

Though Hunter knew she'd feel the pain of the gunshot for the next few weeks, he hardly thought it would keep her from traveling the day trip to town. He raised an eyebrow at her to convey his thought. She averted her eyes, suddenly intent on watching the doctor pack up his bag to leave.

"As always, send someone for me if the pain becomes unbearable or if you feel the wound is becoming infected." Doc turned and sent Hunter a pointed look. "Don't let her tell you otherwise. If you think she's in pain, send for me."

"I'm sitting right here, you know." Tabitha made her annoyance clear.

Doc continued as if she hadn't spoken. "Now if you'll step outside, I'll explain what you need to do the next couple of days to keep the wound clean."

Jason slipped inside while Hunter finished up with Doc. When Hunter reentered her tent, Jason remained stoically near the opening.

"I don't need a caretaker, Hunter. I've been enough of a nuisance to last you both a lifetime. If you'll just leave me alone, I'm sure I'll sleep until morning."

"Not a chance," Hunter replied. "We're both going to sit right here. We'll take turns sleeping if it makes you feel better. The only way you'll get us away from you will be a trip to town at dawn."

"Not a chance." Tabitha mimicked his words.

They were at a standoff, and Hunter motioned for Jason to take the other cot for the first round of sleep. After he settled, Hunter took his place in the chair near the door. Men had been stationed around the dig site to stand watch, each within sight of the next. It wasn't likely anyone would breach that protective line, but Hunter knew he wouldn't sleep well until Tabitha was safely entrusted into her father's care.

"Tabitha, you need to think of the rest of us here. The men won't sleep now that you've been shot. They're having to trade off guard duty." He studied her petite form under the sheet. "You've lost weight since coming here."

If Tabitha could shoot him down with her glare, she would. He ignored her expression.

"Your skirts are so cumbersome that you can't move quickly. You're exhausted. The shooter might not miss next time."

"*If* there's a next time. I don't intend for there to be."

"Did you intend to be shot this time?"

She didn't answer.

"Of course not. You didn't expect it in the least. But even our being prepared won't help. This person is determined. I'm scared for your safety."

Still she remained silent, but hurt permeated her eyes.

His voice softened. "There hasn't been a sign of one fossil or bone. The men are getting weary and tempers are short. As we near the prize, the stakes are getting higher and the price is getting bigger. Your life isn't worth losing over a dinosaur bone, Tab."

"So you want me to sell out like my father." Her voice, devoid of emotion, sounded flat with disappointment.

"No, Tab. I just want you to live."

twelve

A week later, Tab awakened at sunup after another restless night to begin an early day's work in a promising area of their plot. She moved quietly so as not to rouse Hunter when she passed his tent. Judging by his surly mood of late, an extra allotment of sleep would do him good. He'd become worse than a protective mother bear with her cubs.

Her stomach growled in reaction to the enticing aroma of fresh biscuits that wafted over from the dining area, but she tamped down the hunger and forced herself to take advantage of the early morning quiet while she could. Several of the other miners that were left had taken Hunter's lead in blasting through the sturdy sandstone, and the blasts from the cliffs throughout the day were enough to put her already fragile nerves over the edge. She knew Hunter would hustle her over to eat as soon as his feet touched the hard-packed dirt from his cot. He seemed to think a full stomach equated a full recovery, and from his actions he possibly even thought a solid meal would serve as an armor of protection against another bullet attack.

While recuperating she'd stubbornly—according to Hunter—sat on the ground and continued to work a small area she could reach without exerting herself. Meanwhile, her irritable partner concentrated on blasting rock from the equally stubborn—again according to Hunter—wall of rock before them. The effort it took to blow things up seemed to fill a void he had inside. But apparently, in between blasts he still felt it his duty to keep a steady commentary on where all the other annoying situations they'd run up against throughout this dig rated next to her innate refusal to see reason.

She'd found a few fossils the night before and could hardly sleep with the excitement that she finally might be getting close to the find that would end the competition and put Hunter out of his protective misery.

The sound of a rider arriving had her on her feet and shading her eyes from the bright morning sun with her good hand. Too early for the regular supply wagon, she watched as the man slowed and hopped down at the far end of the road. As several other miners staggered out of their tents, she dusted her hand on her skirt and hurried over to see what brought the visitor to the camp at such an early hour.

When the stranger smiled at her and swept his hat from his head, she stopped in surprise. "I have a note for you, ma'am. I was told to deliver it at dawn." He bent the brim of his hat back and forth in his hands. "I figured it must be pretty serious and important for the gentleman to pay me what he did and to want it brought to you so promptly."

"How. . . ?" Tab cleared her throat, which seemed to have closed, whether from the dry morning air or concern, she didn't know. "How do you know it's for me?"

"Well, ma'am," he furrowed his brow in concern, "since you're the only woman here waiting for a letter, I figured I made a pretty good guess." He suddenly stopped fiddling with his hat and reached up to pull a crisp note from his pocket. "Tabitha Augustine. . .is that you?"

She nodded, her heart now battling to join the tightness in her throat. Immediately, she knew something terribly wrong must have happened to her father.

The rider swung back onto his horse and turned to leave as quickly as he'd come.

A few of the more curious miners stood and stared, waiting to see what the fuss was about. Not wanting them to see her reaction if the news didn't bode well, she pushed her way through the crowd and hurried to the privacy of her tent.

Once inside, she tore open the thin paper and read the words scribbled sloppily across the single page. "No, not my Papa. . ."

Tab stared for a long moment at the evil missive clutched tightly in her hands.

A thump against her tent made her jump. "Tabitha? What's all the fuss about? Jason came for me and said you needed me."

Leave it to Jason to feel the need to go for Hunter. She'd have preferred a few more moments alone before having to share the awful news the note contained.

She slowly exited the tent and looked up at Hunter, where her telltale heart paused in its panic and skipped a few beats at the concern written across his handsome face. He took her by the arm and led her to a chair, and his concern grew more evident when she didn't balk at his chivalry.

"The note. It's about my father. A threat." The emotionless voice that escaped from her mouth surprised her. "My father's in danger. I'm to take the next coach from the area and head home. If I do as instructed, my father will stay safe. If I don't, he'll lose the small fortune he won for quitting. . .and. . ." She stared at the ragged holes in the cliff, holes that matched the ones in her heart.

Hunter dropped to his knees and took both of her cold

hands in his, careful not to jostle her hurt arm. "And what, Tab? He'll lose the fortune and what else?"

The gentleness in his cajoling words forced her eyes to look into his. They were dark with concern. "And. . .if I don't go immediately, he'll also lose his life."

❧

Hunter couldn't stand the raw fear he saw in Tabitha's eyes. "Let me pray for you, Tab. It's going to be all right."

She nodded and continued to cling to his hands as he said the soothing words that had the potential to calm her heart.

"I want that peace you have, Hunter. Tell me how. What do I need to do?"

"You have to have faith. You have to believe. God will get you through this."

Her eyes searched his, her fright tearing at his very being. "I don't know how."

"Yes, you do. We've been talking about this for weeks. You've been reading the Bible, right? You need to turn the situation over to God and know that He will bring good out of it. Place your trust in Jesus. Only then will you have peace."

"I have. I prayed the other night that the Lord would lead me, and I told Him I wanted Him to be in charge of all I do. The bullet showed me how fragile life can be. But if He's there, why don't I feel Him? I only feel fear."

"That's to be expected. This is a scary situation. But your faith can carry you through. You have to do as the note instructs. You have to go on faith."

"But how? I don't even know what that means. Help me understand!" Tears of panic gathered in Tabitha's eyes.

"You have faith that if you go to your father as the note instructs, the sender will keep your father from harm, correct?"

"Yes." Tabitha nodded.

Hunter wanted to pull her into his arms and promise he'd make things right. Something he had no business doing. Instead, he focused on his explanation. "You can't know for sure that by obeying the instructions, his captor will keep him safe, but you have to have faith that if you do as you're told, he'll be left alone, do you agree?"

Again she nodded, and one lone tear made a path through the dust on her cheek.

"That's faith, Tab. And you have to believe with the same faith that God will provide for you if you do as the note says. You have no choice but to leave. The supply wagon will be here soon, and you need to be aboard when it pulls back out."

❧

Tab stared at him, though she knew he spoke the truth. He seemed much too eager to be rid of her and hadn't said a thing about accompanying her to town. If he cared as much as he let on, he'd want to be by her side while facing her father's captors, right? It only made sense. But instead, he seemed all too ready to have her on her way. Her suspicion about his motives had her pulling her hands from his gentle grasp. She pushed away the thoughts of faith they'd discussed and instead lashed out at him in the only way she knew—with her words.

"You're on the side of whoever is against me. Why else would you encourage me to give up after all your talk about my father doing the same? You made it clear what you thought of his decision, yet now after I get a mysterious note from a complete stranger, you're more than ready to send me on my way. How do we know this note is legitimate? Maybe it's just a cruel joke."

A shadow of hurt passed across Hunter's face, but she pushed aside her guilt. If he truly was behind the events and note, he most definitely was a good actor. It all felt so confusing.

"Your father made his decision for a price. This is different. Your father is in danger. As I said before, you have no choice. I don't see that you're giving up. You're being blackmailed. Would you really risk your father's safety out of stubborn pride?"

"I can't believe you just said that." She spat the words at him. "How do I know this isn't a ruse to get me off the dig? Look around you. How many others have been chased off? Yet here you stand, untouched."

"I'm not alone. There are a few others. But unless I miss my guess, there will be others threatened once you leave. I'm sure I'll eventually be one of them." He frowned. "This is why I have to stay. You've put up a good fight, but it's past time for you to go. You should have left with your father. If you had, you wouldn't have a bullet hole in your arm right now."

"That sounds suspiciously like a threat. A belated threat."

"How can you say that? I've made my feelings for you very clear. I care about you. I want you safe. Why is that so bad? Can't you even trust me?"

"At this point, I don't feel I can trust anyone. Someone is determined and wants to find those bones."

Hunter yanked off his hat and shoved his hands through his hair in frustration. "We *all* want to find the bones, but not all of us would resort to threats and bribes in order to do so. To have you think so little of me after our time together is inexcusable. And while we're on the subject, for all I know, you and your father could be in cahoots together with this as an outlandish scheme to throw the rest of us off."

"That's preposterous—with our stellar reputations? What would be the point?" Tabitha gasped, and the sound cut sharply through the heated air. "If that's what you think, then I have nothing more to say to you."

She watched for his reaction, and her heart broke a little as he spun around and stalked off in the opposite direction. As soon as the words escaped her mouth, she'd known she shouldn't have said them. But before she could call them back or retrieve them, he'd lashed out at her with his own accusation. And she had to admit, neither one had a reason to trust the other. She really didn't know all that much about him. Now that she thought about it, any attempt to dig too deeply into his background had met with a quick change of topic.

The sound of his open tent flap blowing in the wind caught her attention. He'd taken the liberty to enter her tent on several occasions, yet she'd not once entered his. A small scorpion hovered near the opening. Her approach sent it scuttling inside. As if they moved of their own volition, her feet led her over to the flap, and she peered inside. The area, as sparsely furnished as hers, beckoned to her. She knew she couldn't leave the creature inside, so she hesitantly stepped into the tent. She grabbed a shovel near the doorway and scooped up the offensive critter, tossing him out the entry. The motion dislodged a stack of papers on the nearest crate, and she bent to pick them up. Guilt filled her as she sneaked a peek at the contents, but dismay soon pushed the emotion away.

Several minutes later, she held in her hand proof that he was an active participant and heir to a huge business back

East and that he came from a wealthy family. Everything he'd said he stood for had been a lie. While he talked of his hatred of money, he'd failed to trust her with the fact that he was an heir to a fortune.

❧

Tab waited for Hunter to return then slapped the evidence of his deception into his hands.

"You hate riches and the love of money, yet interestingly enough, according to these documents I just found, you're rich beyond measure." Anger had her gasping for her words. "And to think my father trusted you. I trusted you! To the point I left my father in town and came back here to you! He considered me to be under your protection. How could you do this to me?"

Hunter's expression darkened, and she took a step backward, away from the wrath that slipped across his features.

"And why were you going through my things? You had no right to snoop. You were supposed to be packing to leave."

"Oh, I'll leave all right, as soon as I turn you in to the man in charge. If you would deceive me about your wealth, I'm sure you're capable of deceiving us all these past few weeks. I'm sure Mr. Matthews will be most interested to hear what I have to tell him." She sent him another glare. "To think that you, the man I've come to care about, were the one behind the attacks, the sabotage, and the other incidents. How could I be so foolish?"

"The only thing you're being foolish about is to think such things about me. I thought better of you."

"You thought better of me! How can you say that? I've been up-front with you in every area we've talked about. I didn't hide behind a facade or hide my past. Why wouldn't

I think you were behind all the other cowardly attempts to clear the competition out of your way?" She turned her back to him and hurried toward her tent. She stopped suddenly and swung around, blinking back her tears. "All your explanations about God, about faith. . .I believed them. And I let go, and I believed in you. . . ." Her words broke off again. "How could you?"

She saw devastation, pain, and dismay reflected in his eyes, but his voice was steady as he answered her. "It's all true."

"Yes, thanks for that." At least he admitted the truth when confronted. As much as she hated to admit it, she needed to leave—for her father's sake. Though with Hunter pretty much confessing to everything, surely the bogus note wouldn't matter anymore. But nothing made the past month worth what they'd all gone through. The excitement was gone. The recognition, the thrill of the find, and the ability to choose their own future and have money to cover all their plans dimmed in view of what she'd just learned.

Despondent and angry, she turned to go. Her heart broke more with every step she took away from the man she thought could do no wrong. The man she only now admitted she'd fallen in love with.

એ

Hunter sank to his knees and began to pray. Nothing he'd said had come out the way he'd intended, and apparently she'd taken his words the wrong way. He'd only meant that his teachings about God's love were all true. Not her accusations. He had no idea how she'd translated his negligence to mention he came from a wealthy background to a confession of guilt in the other situations.

He'd really botched things this time. His wealth, always

a thorn in his side, had taken on new dimensions this time. Why hadn't he just come out and opened up to Tabitha about his background and the life he'd endured because of his parents' obsession with money?

"The money always came first with my parents." His words were quiet, but they carried across the early morning air and stopped Tabitha in her tracks. "Just as your father turned his back on you and the dig for a price, no price was ever too high for my parents when it came to turning their back on me. I didn't want to watch you go through the pain that life caused me."

Though she didn't acknowledge him, she stood silent, listening. He whispered another quick prayer for God's guidance. "I'm exactly the man you thought I was, not who you think I am right now. I've done nothing to harm you or anyone else around us."

She turned to look at him, her eyes full of questions.

He stood to face her and moved forward a few steps. "I'm ashamed of my family, of what they stand for. Nothing will stand in their way when they want something. My grandfather made his fortune in mining, and at my earliest opportunity, I moved out here to live with him. He thrives on discovery and adventure, just like me. My family, on the other hand, only thrives on spending my grandfather's funds. And if they were here, I'd not think twice before suspecting them of a deed such as the one you suspect me of, setting up an elaborate ruse so I could bring in this find alone. But I promise you I'm nothing like them." He raised his hands and then dropped them, not knowing what else to say.

"If that's so, why didn't you trust me enough to confide in me? I've shared so much with you. How do I know this isn't more of your deception?"

"My past is my past. I don't consider my family relevant to the here and now. I saw no reason to burden you with things that can't be changed. It wasn't that I didn't trust you enough to share. I just didn't think the story worthy to be shared. I've forgiven my family, but I've moved on. I have a different life now. Unfortunately, my family won't let me go so easily. They had those papers delivered to me here at the site, hoping to entice me back to the family fold."

Tabitha hesitated a moment longer, then shook her head as if to clear it. "I don't know what to think anymore. I don't feel I can trust my own decisions. I'll send for Joey, and we'll let him sort this out."

Hunter's heart fell at her words. Regardless of whether she believed him or not, she'd shut down, and from the look of things, there was no way she'd let her emotions loose for him again.

"I love you, Tabitha." The words were too quiet for her to hear, which he thought best. He felt a gentle nudging to go after her, but he ignored it. He'd only make things worse, and there was no reason to scare her further by chasing her like a desperate man. He paced back and forth in frustration before kicking a large stone with all the venom and frustration he could muster. Instead of the action bringing him release, though, it brought him a searing pain that spread through to his ankle.

"Argh!" The shout of pain went unanswered from any of the men in the nearby tents, and Hunter realized more of the men must have cleared out during the night. He remained alone in his isolated little world.

Footsteps pounded on the packed dirt road, and Hunter

peered through his haze of pain to see Tabitha hurrying his way, her feet throwing tufts of dust up in her wake. "What is it? Have you been harmed? Or is this another ruse to let you have your way?"

When he didn't answer, she stepped closer and stared at him. "Oh."

Apparently the fact that his face contorted in pain clued her in to his dilemma.

He grimaced. "I kicked that rock, and it kicked back harder."

Tabitha glanced at the protruding stone he'd dislodged with his anger. "Well, it might have kicked back, but you cracked it into two pieces. Let's hope it didn't do the same to your foot bone. Here, let me help you stand."

"No!" He pushed her hands away. Her eyes reflected the hurt his rejection caused. "I don't mean no to your help, I only mean, no, don't help me stand right now. Let the pain pass first."

"Then it might really be broken. Let me take a look."

"Not yet. Just let me sit a few minutes." He could feel the sweat bead across his forehead from the stress of holding his tongue. He wanted to let loose with some of the choice words that would have flown out in his younger days. Never had he felt such pain.

"I don't understand." Tabitha drifted over to the upturned rock. "Sandstone is tough, but not so porous as to cause this much pain. What on earth did you kick?" She picked up the innocent-looking stone in her hand.

"A boulder from the feel of it. Just add it to the list of not-so-smart things I've done of late." He gasped. Though the pain had dissipated a bit, the few remaining daggers reverberated up his leg in a most vicious way.

"Are you going to be all right?"

He glanced up as she asked the question. Her tone almost had a laughing quality to it. Surely she wouldn't be callous enough to find humor in the situation. "I'm sure I will be in time." He didn't mask the grumble of frustration.

A short giggle escaped through her clenched lips.

He looked at her in surprise and saw the shock pass over her features.

"I'm so sorry." She looked conflicted as she tried to tamp down her mirth.

If he hadn't been in such pain, he'd find it amusing to watch her try to control her emotions as the laughter defied her and bubbled out.

"This isn't funny at all. I'm not sure what's gotten into me." More horrified giggles. "Oh my!"

Hunter, amid his best efforts not to do so, found himself joining in. "Oh my is right. Not one thing has gone our way during this entire operation. You've been shot, almost crushed by a boulder, accosted in the dark. I might have just broken my foot, but of my own accord. We do make a pair, don't we?"

Tabitha's expression immediately changed, all traces of humor gone. Her voice became a whisper. "We do."

"Tab—"

"Hunter—"

She sank to her knees beside him. "You go first."

"I just wanted to say I'm sorry for everything that's happened." He reached over to pull her hand into his before hurrying to add, "Not that I'm taking credit for any of it, mind you."

"And I wanted to say I'm sorry I doubted you. I know the

man you are inside, and I know in my heart you'd never be able to harm anyone or to deceive others in such a way. I have no excuse for my behavior."

He nodded. "We're both worn out."

"Which means if it's neither of us doing this, someone who means harm to us and my father is still out there. And I still need to leave. Do you think you can stand now?"

"Give me another moment or two, and we'll see. Right now I'm content to sit right where we are." He raised his eyebrows up and down and tightened his grip on her hand.

"Hunter!" Tabitha pulled her hand from his and stood, picking up the broken stone and inspecting it again. "You have me wondering if you're really hurt at all."

"You have my word. I wouldn't fake something like this. I'm definitely hurt." He tugged at her skirt. "Maybe a kiss would make it feel better."

Tabitha narrowed her eyes at him, but the corner of her mouth quirked up and her blue eyes sparkled.

"Or then again, maybe not. From the looks of things, you'd tramp the injured appendage on your way over, just to verify that I'm telling the truth."

"I would at that." She tossed the stone back and forth from one hand to another before laying it next to the other half, then dislodged the other half from where it was embedded into the packed earth. Her hair fell to form a frame around her face, though she'd pulled it back before she'd exited her tent. The emotion of the morning, along with her tendency to run her fingers through it in frustration, allowed tendrils to come loose. Her rapt attention on the rock enabled him to continue the long perusal.

"Hunter. . ." She began to dig into the ground with her

bare hands. She glanced at him with sparkling eyes. "Hunter!" Her breathless voice pulled his attention from where it had lingered while appreciating her pretty profile.

"What?" he absently responded.

"I've found it. The first bone. I'm sure."

"This better not be an attempt to get me to prove my injured foot's ability. . . ." Even as he said the words, he ignored them and made an effort to stand. "Argh." He groaned again.

Since Tabitha didn't even glance his way at his moan of pain, he knew she meant business. He tamped down the pain and crawled over to her side.

She sat back on her heels. "I've done it. *We've* done it. I've never been so happy to see anyone give way to their anger in my life! If you hadn't kicked that rock. . ." She glanced up at him, and the wonder and excitement in her eyes made everything in the past month worthwhile. "We did it."

"Indeed we have." He pulled her close into his embrace, and this time she didn't pull away. Nor did she push him away. "We make a wonderful team."

He leaned toward her, and she closed her eyes, parting her lips as she moved to meet him halfway. He gently brushed his mouth against hers, and they lingered for a moment. When she opened her eyes to look into his, love reflected from their depths.

"You know what we need to do now?" she whispered, reaching up to push a wayward strand of his hair away from his face.

He had several ideas. The first one had to do with trying for another one of her sweet kisses, and the last one ended with thoughts of speaking their wedding vows. He ought to propose first, he guessed.

She tugged away from his grasp and hopped to her feet, brimming with excitement. "We need to get the site coordinator over here to verify the find and record this into the records. Don't go anywhere—I'll be right back."

With a hurt foot, he mused, he couldn't go anywhere. Least of all, as it appeared, to the altar anytime soon.

thirteen

Tab hurried away from Hunter and all the conflicting emotions he brought out in her. When she'd walked a safe distance, she slowed to contemplate the past hour. Her euphoria dimmed as doubt once more consumed her. Had Hunter really hurt his foot? Or was he such a good actor that he'd again conned her into believing something that wasn't true?

But they'd found a bone! That was the important thing for now. Unless. . .her steps slowed again. . .unless he denied her part in the find and took the credit for himself. Surely he wouldn't stoop so low. Her heart skipped a beat. The bone had been found on his claim, his work area. She hated the doubt she felt and suddenly longed for her father. He'd know where to place his trust.

"Have faith." A quiet nudging in her spirit sounded as clearly as if someone stood beside her and whispered into her ear. She glanced around, suddenly aware of the unusual quiet of the camp. By this time things were usually bustling as the men got busy with their work, and dynamite blasts routinely filled the air. Instead, an eerie silence hung over the area, and not one person moved anywhere that Tabitha could see. Jason and the other miners had disappeared from sight. Dark storm clouds hung over the horizon, slowly moving their way.

She hurried her steps. She had to find someone, anyone, other than Hunter. If he were indeed fooling her, she didn't want to be alone with him. The men sometimes went into town on Friday and Saturday nights, but it wasn't usual for them not to return late in the night. If things were this silent on a Saturday morning, she had to assume more of the men had abandoned their claims due to more threats. While their tents remained behind, she noticed that most sites had been cleared of equipment. She knew Jason had to be nearby with the other men she'd seen earlier, but with the early hour, they'd most likely headed back to bed. She'd feel silly if she yelled and brought them running—again—unnecessarily.

A chill passed up Tabitha's back, and she froze in her spot. Hunter was aware that at the moment only she knew about the bone they'd found. She could be in danger if he was the person determined to win at all costs. On the other hand, if it wasn't Hunter who had chased everyone off, she could be in the path of the true villain.

The true villain. . . The words moved across her mind, and she realized with clarity that if she truly felt Hunter were the villain, she wouldn't have had that thought. *Oh Lord, what am I to do? Who do I trust? I feel so alone.*

Again she looked around, feeling as if each tent hid a possible attacker behind it. She needed to get back to Hunter. Together they could figure their way out of this. But with his injury, he'd not be much help if someone confronted them.

"Return to Hunter." A sense of calm settled over her as she felt the guidance in answer to her prayers. She wasn't alone. Hunter was her refuge.

Another thought occurred to her. They hadn't announced their find, so even if someone appeared, they could conceal the bone until help arrived. As it stood, they'd be as safe as possible with that piece of information hidden.

She turned and hurried back toward Hunter's site. She heard voices as she rounded the kitchen tent and darted over to the tent's cover to see whom Hunter spoke with. The two men stood between Hunter's tent and her own, but their voices carried clearly to where she hid.

No, Hunter, don't say it! Of course her silent warning went unheeded. She listened as Hunter told Joey Matthews they'd found the bone, and then he clarified that Tabitha herself had actually found it.

Tabitha felt a peace descend as she realized Hunter hadn't double-crossed her and even went as far as giving her full credit for the find, even though it had been found on his claim. This confirmed what she felt the Lord had told her.

She stepped forward into the company of the men. "Good morning, Mr. Matthews. I'm glad Hunter caught your attention, since I hadn't been able to find you."

Only after her greeting did she notice that Hunter's face had suddenly gone from enthusiastic to wary. And only after she stepped closer did she notice the small gun that Joey clutched in his hand, a gun he aimed directly at Hunter's chest.

"And a good morning to you, too, Miss Augustine." Joey's syrupy smile turned Tabitha's stomach. "You've arrived back just in time. Just in time to save me the trouble of hunting you down, anyway."

His laughter told of a man who had come unhinged.

"Have you shown this bone to anyone else? Or have you told anyone about it?" He turned the gun on Tabitha, and Hunter's face went pale.

Hunter shook his head to silence Tabitha. "Don't be pulling Tabitha into this, Matthews. And since you don't know for sure who all knows about the find, you'd best not do anything rash with either of us."

Joey looked around, and his laughter filled the air. "Right. And with so many witnesses around, there are a lot of prospects whom you could have told."

"But you don't know for sure," Hunter bluffed. "You don't even know for sure when we found the bone. Help could be on the way as we speak."

A touch of doubt crossed Joey's features. "Well then. I guess I'll have to take Tabitha along with me, just to be on the safe side."

"Take her with you where?" Hunter tried to stand, but his foot gave out and he sank back down, his face blanching with pain. "There's no reason for you to take her anywhere." He sagged with resignation. "Listen, leave us alone. You take the bone. Take the credit if you think you can get away with it. I don't care anymore, and I know Tabitha will agree. This isn't worth the trouble it's brought us."

The man obviously wasn't thinking clearly and would never get by with such a stunt, but Tabitha nodded her approval. Joey shook his head. "I can't take the chance you'll change your mind by the time someone else arrives."

❧

Hunter had begun to pray the moment he saw Joey's gun, and he hadn't stopped since. If only he'd pushed harder for Tabitha to understand about God. He felt a measure of peace that she understood about salvation and had truly turned her heart over to God, but more time and talks would have let him know without a doubt. Though he'd never liked Joey, for the first time he realized just how unstable the man seemed to be.

Tabitha was in jeopardy, and Hunter had no way to defend

her. He didn't know how to help. He sent up a plea for intervention. He'd made a mess of things, starting with his omission to Tabitha about his family and ending here, a stubborn holdout when even the hardiest of men seemed to have had the sense to get out while the getting was good.

Again he pushed to his feet, but the pain sent him staggering. He didn't think the foot was broken, but he'd definitely bruised it well. He looked around, but nothing lay within reach for him to use as a crutch.

"Joey, please. We'll sign a statement, a legal affidavit that you're the rightful winner of the contest. Whatever you want us to do. Just please"—he sent a look to Tabitha that he hoped would convey how he felt—"let Tabitha stay with me."

"You've had her eye since she stepped foot here. You think I'm going to hand her over when she's finally mine?" Joey spat. "She's mine, you hear me?"

"I'll *never* be yours, *Mr.* Matthews. I'll die before I let you touch me."

"Don't tempt me, *Miss* Augustine," he hissed. "As I see it, you don't have much choice but to go with me. By the time I'm done with you, you'll be begging for my protection and security."

Tabitha shook her head in terror and backed away. Joey grabbed her roughly by the arm. Hunter lunged forward, disregarding the pain that shot through his foot. But he came up short when the foot gave out, and he found himself flat on his face. Pulling himself along, he inched toward them, but Joey continued to move away, dragging Tabitha along.

Joey stopped long enough to point the gun Hunter's way. Hunter refused to close his eyes, and instead he stared Joey down.

"Lucky for you I don't have more ammunition. With only four bullets left, I'm not inclined to waste any on you. I think the elements and your injury will hurry along your demise. If not, I'll take care of you when I return. Alone."

Hunter sent a message of reassurance to Tab, but it didn't take away the panic in her eyes. Somehow he'd find a way to rescue her, *before* the deranged man harmed her. He continued to send up pleas to God. He knew there were others somewhere nearby. Joey apparently thought otherwise.

"On second thought," Joey stopped and lifted his gun Hunter's way. "I think I will risk one bullet and take one shot."

Hunter stared him down and watched as Joey pulled the trigger. Tabitha screamed, and he felt the bullet graze the side of his head. A mix of blood and sweat dripped into his eyes, but he wiped it away and watched as Joey yanked Tabitha around the tent and out of his sight. The man was insane. And, thank heavens, a lousy shot. The bullet had barely scratched the surface of Hunter's skin. Like any minor head wound, the bleeding had already slowed after a momentary trickle. He fought the urge to laugh in his enemy's face. He knew the action would only fuel the crazy man's fire. An angry rumble of thunder sounded to the west, and with the scent of rain heavy in the air, he lowered his head in defeat.

God, please help me. There has to be a way. You can do a miracle on my foot. He gingerly tested it, but the pain shot through as intense as ever. *Then send someone, God, please. Please bring Tabitha to safety. If nothing else, let her come to know You before she comes to harm.*

He pulled himself along the ground toward his tent, determined to get his guns. He stopped when he heard what sounded like hoofbeats in the distance. *No, God, please! If Joey leaves by horseback, I'll never be able to catch them. Not in this condition.*

After listening a moment longer, he realized the hoofbeats were nearing the camp, not going away from it. He looked around for cover. He wouldn't make it to the tent in time. If Joey had decided to use up any more of his bullets, he'd make sure he wasn't an easy target. He pulled his body along the ground and swung behind Tabitha's tent just as the first raindrop fell.

"Hello there!" A familiar voice called out, and Hunter's heart leaped with gratitude at God's quick answer to his prayer.

"Over here, behind your tent."

Hunter had never been so glad to see anyone in his life, especially since his rescuer turned out to be Tabitha's father. Dr. Augustine rounded the canvas side, and alarm filled his features.

"What on earth has happened to you?" He leaned down and hoisted Hunter to his feet, or foot in this case.

Balancing against the surprisingly strong older man, Hunter half hopped while Dr. Augustine half carried him over to his beloved chair.

"Joey Matthews happened to me. He's the one behind the threats and the danger, and now he has Tabitha."

"Which direction did they go?"

Hunter pointed.

"Were they on foot?"

"I believe so. The only horse I heard turned out to be yours. You're the answer to my prayers."

"Well now, I don't know about that, but I do know I'm going to rescue my daughter."

"In all due respect, sir, do you think that's a good idea? You've barely had time to recuperate from your heart ailment."

Tabitha's father pulled himself to his full height. "I'm plenty young enough to take care of my daughter's captor. But with both of us on their trail, he surely won't have a chance to better us."

"But my foot. . ."

Hunter watched as the man walked into the tent and returned with a walking stick. "Carry this along. You'll ride the horse, and I'll walk alongside. We're going to get my daughter."

Gingerly, Hunter put pressure on his wounded foot, relieved that the walking stick sufficiently diverted the pain.

Jason stumbled out of his tent. "What's going on? I thought I heard a gunshot but saw the dark clouds when I looked. I figured it was thunder."

"Joey Matthews has Tabitha. Round up any of the remaining men and follow us." Hunter continued to move as he talked. He swung up on the horse and, after the older man retrieved Hunter's weapons from his tent, motioned Dr. Augustine in the direction he'd last seen Tabitha as she'd been dragged along by Joey.

❧

Terror didn't begin to cover the emotion Tabitha felt at being alone with Joey. Though he wasn't a big man, he still towered over her by several inches. Not to mention the fact that she knew he carried a gun. A gun he'd already shot her with once. And the gun he'd just used to shoot Hunter in the head.

"You've all ruined this for me. It's your own fault you're in this situation."

His words angered her. "Our fault? We came and did what

was expected of us. You're the one who misused your power."

"I'm always the one who has to set things up on these digs. I do all the preliminary work and oversee everything. Yet it's the scientists and archaeologists who get all the praise and credit and acclaim. This time, though, will be different. This time the credit will be mine, even if I have to dispose of you, Hunter, and even your father when the poor man arrives to check on you. Most of the others took their warnings to heart and cleared out. Even your own father listened, but you"—he used the butt of the gun to push his hat up away from his eyes—"you had to stick around with your sweetheart."

She started to interrupt that Hunter wasn't her "sweetheart," but when she contemplated his words, she realized Joey correctly summarized their relationship.

She had no idea if Hunter had survived. She'd only had time to see a trickle of blood, and then Hunter's head dipped down to rest on his arms. Joey had jerked her around before she could assure herself of his safety. But she had a small inkling of hope since Joey had just mentioned his *future* intent to kill them all. Then again, who could trust the words of a madman? Though she'd uttered a few awkward prayers so far, for the first time ever, she felt a strong inner desire to pray. *Please, God, hear my prayer and keep watch over Hunter until help comes. Please help us find our way out of this situation, a situation all my worldly knowledge added up together can't fix.*

Continuously she said her silent prayers, and peace descended upon her. God had been there for them so far, and she felt sure in her heart He'd continue to be there for them as this all played out. How He'd intervene, she had no idea. But she knew deep inside that even if worst came to worst, she'd have a place in heaven next to her dear grandmother. That thought alone lifted her spirits. Hunter, bless him, had brought her to this realization and knowledge. She reassured herself that the peace of knowing Jesus surpassed all fear she'd felt moments before. Whatever her future held, she had peace in knowing she wasn't alone and that God walked along beside her.

"You're finding humor in this situation?"

Joey's voice, full of contempt, interrupted her musings. Tabitha realized a small bubble of laughter had passed over her lips. Though she knew she wasn't out of jeopardy, she had faith everything would be okay. God was watching out for her.

Her mouth curved up into a smile as she looked Joey full in the eyes for the first time since they'd left camp. "Not humor, Joey, but peace. God has given me the most incredible peace."

fourteen

Hunter led the way and followed the markings in the dust where Tabitha had dragged her feet. She'd done a good job of leaving a trail, if the rain cooperated and didn't wash the remnants away. As usual, the rain had stopped after a quick drizzle passed over them. The humidity remained, and thunder continued to rumble above. A few bolts of lightning caused him concern for their safety now that they were without the protection of the bluffs.

They'd taken a moment to grab some other weapons, which included sticks of dynamite. But he had no idea how they'd get close enough to do much good before alerting Joey of their presence. Their gun wouldn't do much good as long as Joey had Tabitha as a shield.

After hearing a noise to the west, Hunter turned his head in that direction and tensed as a cloud of dust moved their way.

"What is that, a dust storm?" he asked, eyes squinted against the dimness brought on by the storm.

"Nope. It's reinforcements." Dr. Augustine didn't even try to hide the delight in his voice. "I rounded 'em up before I left town. Some of the men filled me in last night about the latest threats. Most of them decided at the last moment to carry out what they could, while leaving the tents behind for later. I reminded them my Tabitha had also remained behind. They couldn't remember if they'd seen you all at the impromptu meeting. This morning, at sunup, I reminded them of all the sweet things my daughter had done for them throughout the past month and asked if any of them would want her loss of life on their conscience."

He glanced at the oncoming stampede and sent Hunter a grin. "Apparently, they decided they didn't."

Another cloud of dust from the south showed that Jason had succeeded in rounding up some other men who had stayed in the camp and the extra horses.

"Yeehaw!" Hunter spurred the horse on, though he made sure his cry of glee was a soft one. No way would he alert Joey to the oncoming mass of angry scientists. No telling what he'd do. Besides, he wanted to personally see the look on the man's sorry face when he registered the wronged men had all banded together against him, as they should have from the start.

The riders pulled up short, towing along an extra mount that hastily found its way to Dr. Augustine's side.

Jason's grim smile preceded his words. "I brought 'im along for Miss Augustine, but apparently you can use him more."

"You all sure are a sight for sore eyes." Hunter slapped Jason on the back. "Thanks for coming to help us. Joey has about half an hour on us, but they're on foot, so we should catch up in no time."

"We're mighty glad to help." Jason spoke for them all, but the other men nodded their agreement. "It's a sad day to find out our trusted overseer has betrayed the position he's been given and is behind all the threats. And to think he's sunk so low as to kidnap Tabitha. There's never a finer lady to walk the earth if you ask me. We've been braggin' to her father each time we met up in town. We're happy to help."

Each man muttered his own thought as to what should be done to the renegade site coordinator when they caught up with him. They wanted to be sure and punish him for taking Tabitha away from them.

Hunter didn't bother to point out that the majority of them had silently abandoned Tabitha and him the night before without an apparent backward glance. But they'd come back today to bring Joey to justice. That's all that mattered now. He swung his own horse around and began to trail the prints at a much faster pace now that Dr. Augustine had his own mount.

☙

Tabitha pretended to stumble again, digging her boots into the ground as deeply as she could, which earned her another hard jerk from Joey. Her arm would be bruised and swollen tomorrow, if tomorrow ever came.

"Can we stop a moment? I'm thirsty, and I need to rest."

"We'll rest soon enough. See that cliff up ahead? That's as far as we're going."

Suddenly her desire to rest came second to her desire to stay alive and on the move. If they stopped, she had no idea what would happen. The few things she could think of didn't make her feel like reaching that destination anytime soon.

She felt much safer out here, in the open, where Hunter could see her if he found a way to reach her—if he was even alive. The thought brought tears to her eyes. If Hunter had died from the gunshot, there would be no rescue. She pushed the upsetting notion away. She feigned a faint, which earned her another jerk.

"If you continue to yank on me in such a way, you're going to pull my arm right out of the socket."

Joey snickered. "If you'd stop dawdling, I wouldn't need to urge you on."

"I can't help it if the weather and upset is causing me to swoon. I'm sure my fainting would dampen your plans a bit.

Surely you want me to remain alert for the afternoon of terrors you have planned."

"Not necessarily." Joey shrugged. "I'll follow through on my plans whether you're alert or unconscious. It makes no matter to me." He leered over at her. "Though I must admit, having you awake will make my plans more fun."

Tabitha felt sick to her stomach. They approached the cliffs, and the queasiness intensified with every step nearer they took.

"There. In that little alcove to our right, that's where I'll take you."

In her mind, his words could mean either of two things, neither of them pleasant. Did he intend to have his way with her before he killed her? Or did he mean to kill her outright? She felt pretty sure he planned to go with the first horrible scenario that had come to her. The thought made bile rise up into her throat.

With sudden clarity of thought, she pushed her hat from her head and let it drop to the ground as they diverted from their previous path and headed for the bluffs. Joey, focused as he was on where they were going, didn't even notice.

She couldn't hold her silence a moment longer. "What do you have planned for me?"

He turned to her with glazed eyes. "You'll find out soon enough."

Tabitha decided to make the decision for herself. "What you won't do is lay a hand upon me."

Digging her feet into the ground for what she figured would be the last time, she refused to move a step farther.

"Is that right? I seem to have the gun, and you seem to be defenseless. Common sense says you'd be prudent to stay quiet and do exactly as I say."

Tabitha let out a sardonic laugh. "The ironic thing about that is that common sense has never been one of my stronger attributes. Ask anyone who knows me. It seems that book knowledge, even when it comes easy for a person, doesn't assure that a person will have the slightest hint of common sense."

He jammed the gun into her side, and she forced herself not to react. "You have three bullets left. One more for me, one more for Hunter, and one for anyone else who might come to find out what's happened to us. I don't think you'll waste one on maiming me for a thrill."

"You're more trouble than you're worth. I'm going to enjoy putting this bullet into you at close range."

Tabitha stood tall. "Then please do it quickly and put us both out of our misery. I don't want to spend another moment in your company, and if death is what it takes to avoid that, I'll gladly embrace it."

Raw fury took over Joey's countenance. "You'll not rush me into anything. I'm making the decisions now, remember? You might not have come to me willingly, but you'll go out only after I've gotten what I want from you."

He threw her to the ground and grabbed a handful of her tan skirt. She fought him with all she was worth.

"You will not win!" she screamed. "Not in this. I can't stop you from killing me, but you will not lay a hand upon me before doing so."

A hard slap across the face was her reward for standing up to him.

She spit at him and laughed. She wanted to provoke him enough to make him shoot her. She knew she couldn't get away, but she could ensure he sent her on to Glory before defiling her body in such a disgusting way. She would die first. She had to.

He again grabbed her skirts, and again she fought him off. Her arm throbbed where the bullet had entered, but she couldn't take time to worry about that. Besides, the pain kept her more focused on her mission.

Another hard slap had her seeing stars. She smiled. Soon it would all be over. Joey screamed his outrage at her contempt, but before he could lay another hand upon her, a horse seemingly appeared from out of nowhere and jumped over them at full speed. Hunter leaped from the saddle midair and landed full force on Joey. He didn't stop punching him until her father pulled the enraged man aside.

"That's enough, son."

Hunter stood with fists clenched, breathing hard, unaware that in his fury he balanced on one foot while obliviously babying the other. Dried blood on his temple showed the remnant of his run-in with Joey's gun. His filthy shirt, torn in several places, hung from his shoulders. Tabitha had never seen a more beautiful sight in her life.

She only tore her eyes away from him when her father bent down and pulled her into his arms. "Are you all right? Did he hurt you?"

"I'll be fine now." As her emotions died down, her body began to shake with shock. She watched as the men removed the gun from Joey, draped him over a horse, and secured the crazed man face down.

Only after being assured the man could do her no more harm did she feel safe enough to throw her arms around her father. "Oh, Papa. I'm so glad you're here."

"I'm sorry I wasn't here already. I never should have left you.

Can you find it in your heart to forgive me for my actions?"

She pulled away and searched his eyes. "Your safety and spiritual life are more important to me than anything else."

He looked confused.

"I talked to God, Papa, and I've turned my life over to Him. I felt a peace like I can't describe throughout this whole ordeal. I know it sounds crazy to you, and I know where you stand in your beliefs, but will you promise me you'll listen later when things settle down and we have a chance to talk? Will you keep an open mind to my words and let me have my say?"

A thoughtful expression crossed his face. "I would, but. . ." He glanced at Hunter and smiled. "Hunter asked if I'd pray with him on the way out here. I knew I needed the faith and determination he has. He said he only had that because of his faith and belief in God. I've spent my time in town well. I've attended church with Bitsy, and we've had a lot of talks about faith and salvation during the past three weeks. Hunter only had the few moments to share, but his faith solidified my new understanding. All that said, I'm working on making my peace with God."

"Oh, Papa! That's the best news I've heard in a long time."

"Well, Jesus has certainly been my greatest find." Her father laughed out loud. "The journey for riches—the big 'find' we've searched for all these years—has been unfulfilling and left a void. But this latest find—Jesus and all He has to offer us—well, with that realization, I know my adventure of seeking to grow closer to Him will prove to be a greater joy than all my former quests combined. I'm glad you'll be on the journey with me."

"Always, Papa. As you stated so eloquently, the journey to grow closer to Christ will indeed be our greatest find."

epilogue

Hunter smiled with gratitude as he and Tabitha stepped forward to accept the plaque from the Statford Museum curators. Then, in unison, they turned to hand it over to her father. Dr. Augustine stepped up and smiled when he saw all three of their names engraved upon it.

"We're blessed to have you join us on such a special day." Hunter addressed the small crowd gathered for the occasion. "As you know, we'll be starting the actual excavation next week, and we'd be honored to have each one of you, those who stuck things out when the going got rough, to join us in the work laid out before us."

His announcement was welcomed by cheers.

"You'll be paid nicely for your time by the museum, unlike the free month you 'donated' not too long ago."

Chuckles—and more cheers—rang out around them.

Hunter turned to Tab, who looked radiant in a long, white silk gown. She'd decorated her hair with tiny flowers for the occasion. Her blue eyes sparkled as they met his. "And Tab, I can't imagine a bigger challenge than working with you."

"Amen!" several voices called out from the crowd. Tabitha sent them a playful glare before turning her sweet smile his way.

He continued his spiel. "I want you by my side—forever."

"Get on with the important part!" Jason's voice rose above the others. "You think we came all this way to watch you get an award or to watch your sappy interlude with Tabitha?"

This time it was Hunter's turn to quiet the rowdy crowd with a look. He turned to the preacher behind them.

The man stepped forward and said the words that joined Hunter's and Tabitha's lives into one. Hunter didn't wait for the final proclamation before pulling a startled Tabitha against him for a long, slow kiss. She returned the kiss with passion, apparently forgetting that anyone other than the two of them existed. Only after her father cleared his throat rather loudly did Tabitha seem to remember their guests. Mortified, she glanced at the crowd. Hunter followed her gaze and noticed there wasn't a dry eye in the bunch.

The crusty old miners and scholarly scientists all had different excuses for their softhearted reactions. "I seem to have gotten some dust in my eye."

"I've been under the weather ever since that last storm roared through. My eyes have been watering ever since."

"Oh right, the storm that only brought a few drops of rain?" *Snort.* "Of course."

"That rock chipped that one day and flew up to nick my eye. I must have irritated it again standing out here in this hot sun."

Tabitha couldn't hold back her laughter as she listened to their ruminations. "Seems all sorts of ailments have fallen upon our workers; we'd best go easy on them in the future."

"Seems so." Hunter pulled her close again as the crowd dispersed and went their separate ways. "But for now, the only future I'm concerned about is the one we're about to begin together."

He surprised her by swinging her off her feet and up into his arms. Her father appeared with a horse and wagon in front of the makeshift stage where they'd received their plaque and held their wedding ceremony. "Your chariot awaits."

After carrying her down the stairs, Hunter deposited her gently on the wooden bench seat before climbing up to join her. He lifted the reins and nodded to the men who'd stopped to watch their retreat. "We'll see you all soon."

Hunter watched the look that Tabitha and her father exchanged. Though they'd see him later in town, she suddenly leaned down and gave the man a teary hug. Bitsy, standing at Tabitha's father's side, received a hug of her own.

They waved good-bye and were on their way. Tabitha snuggled close against his side.

"Well, Tab, I have to ask. Was the dig everything you hoped it to be?"

Tabitha threw her head back and let her laugh carry on the wind. "Everything and more, as I'm sure you know. The greatest find: Jesus. The most fun find: the bone." The expression in her eyes softened as her mouth tipped up in the spontaneous grin he found so endearing. "And the most unexpected find: you."

He leaned down and kissed her. "Here's to many more finds in our future."

"Amen to that," she agreed. "Our adventures have just begun."

A Letter To Our Readers

Dear Reader:

In order that we might better contribute to your reading enjoyment, we would appreciate your taking a few minutes to respond to the following questions. We welcome your comments and read each form and letter we receive. When completed, please return to the following:

Fiction Editor
Heartsong Presents
PO Box 719
Uhrichsville, Ohio 44683

1. Did you enjoy reading *The Greatest Find* by Paige Winship Dooly?
   ❑ Very much! I would like to see more books by this author!
   ❑ Moderately. I would have enjoyed it more if

   _____

   _____

   _____

2. Are you a member of **Heartsong Presents**? ❑ Yes ❑ No
   If no, where did you purchase this book? _____

   _____

3. How would you rate, on a scale from 1 (poor) to 5 (superior), the cover design? _____

4. On a scale from 1 (poor) to 10 (superior), please rate the following elements.

   ____ Heroine   ____ Plot
   ____ Hero   ____ Inspirational theme
   ____ Setting   ____ Secondary characters

5. These characters were special because? _____

_____

_____

6. How has this book inspired your life? _____

_____

_____

7. What settings would you like to see covered in future
   Heartsong Presents books? _____

_____

_____

8. What are some inspirational themes you would like to see
   treated in future books? _____

_____

_____

9. Would you be interested in reading other **Heartsong
   Presents** titles? ☐ Yes ☐ No

10. Please check your age range:
    ☐ Under 18   ☐ 18-24
    ☐ 25-34   ☐ 35-45
    ☐ 46-55   ☐ Over 55

Name_____

Occupation _____

Address _____

City, State, Zip_____

S choolmarm Grace Calhoun
has her work cut out for her
with the Reeves boys—five
malicious monsters of mayhem
who are making her life
miserable. Things couldn't get
any worse. . .or could they?

Historical, paperback, 288 pages, 5³/₁₆" x 8"

Please send me ____ copies of *Calico Canyon*. I am enclosing $10.97 for each.
(Please add $3.00 to cover postage and handling per order. OH add 7% tax.
If outside the U.S. please call 740-922-7280 for shipping charges.)

Name_____

Address _____

City, State, Zip _____

To place a credit card order, call 1-740-922-7280.
Send to: Heartsong Presents Readers' Service, PO Box 721, Uhrichsville, OH 44683

Heartsong

Presents

Great Inspirational Romance at a Great Price!

Heartsong Presents books are inspirational romances in contemporary and historical settings, designed to give you an enjoyable, spirit-lifting reading experience. You can choose wonderfully written titles from some of today's best authors like Wanda E. Brunstetter, Mary Connealy, Susan Page Davis, Cathy Marie Hake, Joyce Livingston, and many others.

When ordering quantities less than twelve, above titles are $2.97 each.
Not all titles may be available at time of order.

SEND TO: Heartsong Presents Readers' Service
P.O. Box 721, Uhrichsville, Ohio 44683
Please send me the items checked above. I am enclosing $ _____
(please add $3.00 to cover postage per order. OH add 7% tax. WA add 8.5%). Send check or money order, no cash or C.O.D.s, please.
To place a credit card order, call 1-740-922-7280.

NAME _____

ADDRESS _____

CITY/STATE _____ ZIP_____